GEORGE

Ophelia Finsen

Also by Ophelia Finsen:

Lovers of Old Films
This is Living
Society of Lost Causes
The Women of Jimanac
Skye
The Romanian
At the Upper Villa Tyde
Perception
You Stole My Thunder
Bella Donna

ISBN: 978-0-9934120-3-5

Even in West Yorkshire, where it rained more often than it did not, and literature recorded cold winds howling mournfully across the moors, the locals were suffering from a heat wave. The clouds had departed for a more comfortable climate. The sun had full power-blasting access to the Victorian industrial town nestled between woodland and hills. People were baked slowly in their own sweat; a slow, torturous marinade whilst flesh crispened and crackled. Hair frizzed and frazzled. In the more active it stuck unflatteringly to skin in rivulets of sweat.

Bronte Campbell was slumped on the settee in the stance of a limp and maimed starfish, staring dumbly at the silent television screen. It was at times like this, on an evening after work with the house thermostat gleefully announcing 28 degrees Celsius, that she understood she was a northerner. As much as she hated the snow and ice, she had ways of coping. With the heat she felt as though the end was nigh.

She'd ventured to the shops after work, sweating her way up the hill with the uncomfortable feeling of heat off the street paving radiating up her skirt. Her sunglasses kept slipping down her face, and out of the corner of her eye she could see a fat droplet of sweat hanging off her nose ring. Diamonds of sweat. Hardly glamorous.

Food had been the sensible requirement, and she had gathered a few items, most of which were now abandoned on the work surface in the kitchen. The bunch of bananas was rapidly ripening in the plastic bag. On the walk up, all she'd thought about was a cheap washing up bowl. Ignoring the people fighting over the last electric fans, she'd found a new washing up bowl and gleefully taken it home. Once filled with cold water and set on the floor, it was the perfect receptacle for her hot swollen feet. They looked more like the bloated remains of a rotting corpse than the dainty feminine feet she supposed she ought to have.

A fly buzzed around the light fitting before landing on Bronte's knee. She could feel its legs, light as feathers, scampering over her skin. Instinctively she lashed out and flattened the fly on her leg. She grimaced when she saw the mashed insect on her hand.

"Christ," she muttered, wiping her hand on her skirt and thinking that would have to go in the wash tonight. She lent her head back on the settee and stared up at the ceiling where another four flies were chasing each other around the lampshade. One of the farms outside of town had decided to have a clear out, so the rumours went, of a shed where a lot of animal waste had been left too long. That and the heat had been a neat breeding ground for maggots, and the overdue spring clean had disturbed a fly population reaching plague levels. With their environment destroyed, they had headed for the little town, in the hope of dirty unwashed plates to scrabble upon and double glazed windows to smash into. She had one of those fly-paper-in-a-tube contraptions hanging from the kitchen ceiling with about thirty flies stuck on, some not quite dead. And yet they continued to come.

One of the flies above gave up on the chase and came down to buzz around Bronte's head. "Fuck off!" She lethargically batted at it when it came too close to her ear. The change in air movement, or rather the appearance of air movement, sent the fly spinning. It became entangled in Bronte's hair, and the buzzing increased in panic. Bronte yelped and jumped up, splashing water all over the living room floor. Wrenching her hair grips out of her up do, she leant forward and with the best of the head bangers, started shaking her chestnut locks, desperately trying to get the insect away from her. The fly was released and plopped onto the carpet.

Bronte sank back onto the sofa, her face flushed and her breathing heavy. She had never been good with creepy crawlies.

Her morning ritual followed the same pattern. The heat wave changed little other than that the curtains remained closed as if it were a house of mourning. Keep the heat out. It matched the winter response, when the curtains remained closed to keep in the heat. It never seemed to do the job either way yet a window without curtains was unthinkable.

Whilst singing to the radio and looking at herself in the large mirror over the mantelpiece, Bronte selected earrings for the day. It was a Wednesday, which meant streak morning, and she drew a line in the dust on the mantelpiece alongside all the previous weekly streaks. At this rate she ought to have dusted the mantelpiece by autumn, at which point, rather like the Forth Rail Bridge, she'd have to start all over again. She'd never been one for domestics and struggled to keep her attention on the job of running a house. More essential factors such as clean clothes, cooking and the dishes got done, but beyond that there seemed to be far more important things in life than dusting, wiping, hovering, polishing... her internal grumbling paused as the song got to the chorus, and she skipped around the living room to head for the kitchen at the back of the house.

Bronte was the original early bird, and had time to do things before she had to go to work. It helped that she didn't need to be at work until half nine, but even so, she liked to laze in bed with the radio, take time getting ready, eat breakfast and do a little drawing before earning a living. With such a list of requirements, a girl needed to be up with the sun.

She lived in a two bedroom terrace house built in the Victorian age and bequeathed to her by a great aunt. It was a popular part of town to live in, what with it being considered of world heritage status. Given her minimum wage job and low aspirations, single-girl status of lowly heritage, without the last will and testament of said great aunt, she would never had amassed the financial wealth necessary to be a home owner anywhere, let alone in the picturesque hallowed streets of Saltaire. She'd been here four years and was gradually renovating to suit her own tastes. It was slow work, and like the Forth Rail Bridge and the mantelpiece dust, by the time it was all complete, the first features would be falling apart again.

Whilst eating breakfast she would sit on a stool by the kitchen window and sketch her small walled back yard. The same view every day, but with each day's sketch she might take on a particular plant or piece of architectural salvage she had collected, or the garden as a whole. The idea was to capture the passing seasons of her home. At work she'd put out all the postcards of the art exhibition of a seasonal study of a lane in Yorkshire, and had been inspired with the idea of yet another project. Bronte drew and painted and modelled with silver clay and knitted and crocheted and had more ideas for projects then she would have days on this earth. Rather like the Forth Rail Bridge, the mantelpiece dust and her house renovating, the work would never be done. And that was probably the best definition of Bronte: a lot of good ideas, but hardly anything ever seen all the way through.

She was using oil pastels to catch the shimmer of sunlight on the leaves of the overhanging tree from next door. Looking back into the kitchen she caught sight of the kitchen clock and spilled the contents of her pastel box over the floor in surprise. It was twenty past nine.

"Shit." Bronte stumbled to her feet, tossing the sketch pad onto the kitchen table. She went to arrange her lunch, then decided better of it when she saw her grubby fingers. She went to wipe them on one of the tea towels, then remembered the last time she'd done so, and that she'd never gotten the marks out of the fabric. Be sensible, she told herself, squirting washing up liquid onto her hands and lathering up to a furious cloud of cleanliness. Wiping her hands dry on her skirt, the tea towel already forgotten, she rushed in putting her lunch together. A couple of bananas were ripped off the bunch and, together with half a pack of rice cakes and a yoghurt out of the fridge, were lobbed into a cloth bag.

Bag, house keys and sunglasses were waiting by the front door and she was ready to go. A last minute thought of a pencil and a Burmese hair pin were grabbed on her way out to twist up and hold her hair in place and she was out of the building, strands of hair already coming loose. Bronte only lived a five minute walk from work, and yet most mornings she cut her arrival painfully close. At one time she had gone home for lunch, but distractions at home had meant she had been late back on several occasions. From experience and the stern look of the bookshop manager she had decided it was probably best she didn't leave the building until it was the end of the school day.

The bookshop in question had been paying the bills for the past four years. It wasn't immediately what one would have thought of as a bookshop, situated on a high-ceiling endless floor. The shelves had rolled in as the balls of wool and remnants of a fabrics industry had rolled out. Goodbye British manufacturing. Hello intellectualism. The old mill building, the iconic mother in the old town, stood by the river and canal, seemingly towering up out of the water itself. The bookshop was on the second floor, filled with endless rows of bookshelves. Most subjects were catered for, all with full priced, pristine brand new books that Bronte usually couldn't afford. She could wax lyrical to the customers about buying new, supporting local, and loving paper over digital readers but in personal preference she was a savvy shopper of the internet and second hand.

She had artistic, 'artisan' handwriting as the shop manager, Lillian O'Keefe, would say. Bronte had the task of writing up the weekly book recommendations. They had a shelf with personalised recommendations from the staff, with a little block of text on why that book had changed their views on life (views that changed so frequently it was a surprise none of them suffered from chronic dizzy spells). Staff was allowed to read new stock on the express understanding that spines were not to be creased and pages not to be folded. Thoughts were duly scrawled on lined paper and Bronte would write them up, hoping she deciphered some of the more illegible hands correctly. Even if she didn't have the money to support such independent enterprises as much as she would have liked, it was a nice bookshop as far as new stock could go. For nothing could capture the spirit of a second hand bookshop as far as Bronte was concerned. Not that she would ever admit such a thing to Lillian.

Hands moved across the desk, drumming out a beat.

"Morning, Robert," Bronte said without looking up.

"Bronte," the man greeted her. He was always bored at work when there was nothing to do, no customers to talk to, talk at, bore on the subject of jazz or Yorkshire life. Robert was nearing fifty, wiry and a silver fox. Always immaculately dressed in that deceptively smart-casual Edwardian country work wear that was en vogue and far too expensive. He always turned up to work in shirts and waistcoats of sombre woollen colours.

"Writing the recommendations."

"That's what it looks like," she said flatly, still not looking up at him. Putting down her pen, she took a green felt tip to add some flourishes to the first word.

"Always engrossed in your work. You're lucky you can use your real calling here."

Bronte gave a little sigh and finally met his gaze. "Writing little cards to stick on shelves is hardly meeting my artistic potential."

"It's something."

"Lillian said no to your CDs again?"

He looked disgruntled. "Yes. She's let me put them on a corner shelf but she will not play them in the shop. We've just got to listen to this." He waved his hand dismissively in the air.

"That's life."

"Don't be so defeatist."

"Me? I'm not the one grumbling about the music."

"No, but we can't just accept everything as it is. You must want more out of life."

Bronte closed her eyes and put her hands flat down on the desk. Give me strength, she thought. It is too early in the morning. Robert wasn't coping with the fact he was turning 50 this year, and was desperately trying to impart wisdom on all of his younger colleagues as if no one else had discovered the purpose of life yet.

She opened her eyes and he was still there. "Don't you have a till to mind?"

"You're stood there."

"I'm writing. Besides, I've got tags to bluetack to shelves." She gathered up the cards and left the customer island in the middle of the shop. Thank god for Wednesday morning chores. It was too early to listen to other people's woes.

Eleven o'clock found her at the side of the floor where the sun hadn't reached, gazing out of the window wistfully. She'd been putting out some new books, and ought to head back for the tills but that would mean standing in sunshine and she wasn't ready to take the heat. Robert was loitering there, still wearing his woollen waistcoat. Did he not feel the heat? Perhaps he was a type of lizard man, she pondered, needing the heat to produce his energy.

She drew a hand over her forehead, scowling at the film of sweat that her fingers removed.

Early afternoon when the lunch rush had finished, found Bronte manning the central till on her own. She was hunched over the desk at an uncomfortable angle, trying to shield the fact that she was reading one of the expensive art magazines they stocked. She could never afford to buy these high brow publications, but loved the photography and imagery. She'd carefully page through a copy, taking a few days on each magazine before sliding it to the bottom of the pile.

"I really want you to make me this."

She jumped; a flash of guilty panic as she pushed the magazine under a pile of paper bags. A printed pamphlet had been slapped down on the desk amongst the stands of whimsical magnets, pens and postcards. On the front there was a head shot of a man wearing a stripy woollen bobble hat and a disturbing homemade beard. A knitting pattern for quirkier head gear.

"Well, you could run that up easy, like, what?"

The woman on the other side, Eileen, with dark hair knotted up on her head and carefully made up scarlet lips, didn't look as though she'd just finished the lunch time shift in the diner at the other end of the converted mill's second floor. She was neither sweaty nor distressed. Bronte supposed it was something about still being in her twenties that made Eileen energetic, flawless and incapable of putting weight on. Although she couldn't remember having been that perfect when she'd still been in her twenties.

"I've started seeing this guy."

"Another one?"

Eileen shrugged off the surprise. "You've got to try a few, shop around. This one's a bit different though. Bit of a nerd. He's at uni, in Leeds. Doing his masters."

Bronte picked up the knitting pattern and flicked it open. It didn't look to be particularly complicated.

"He's got a bit of a weird sense of humour."

"Anyone thinking about woollen clothing in this heat is a bit weird."

"Well, that's not the weirdest thing. You'll never guess what he studies."

"I don't know. Beardology?"

"Bronte!"

"Sorry. What's he doing? His master of beards?"

"He studies entomology, well, zoology, insects and bugs, you know, that sort of thing. Apparently entomology isn't the right term anymore because he studies slugs and that's malacology..." Eileen snorted up her laughter. "Listen at me, I have been paying attention. It must be love."

"You're seeing a guy who studies slugs?" Bronte didn't sound as though she could quite believe it. Aside from the fact that anything connected to slugs was revolting and ought to be avoided, intellectualism and specialisation wasn't usually something that attracted Eileen. Especially when it involved the outdoors. She was a quick fix girl who got bored with horrific speed. She got through men almost as many times as she brushed her hair.

"I know, you wouldn't think it. I'm not usually into academics. Especially ones into bugs." She rolled her eyes. "But he's really into his thing. It's interesting to listen to him talk. Sounds like they're a right mad bunch. The head of department's into beetles. That's called Coleopterology..."

"Those are big words you've been learning."

"And his dissertation tutor is this insane guy who studies arachnids and has this crazy beard."

Bronte closed her eyes. Of all of the bugs in the world, spiders were the ones she couldn't stand. She was terrified, literally paralysed when one of those eight legged beasts dared to set its many feet into her living space. The mention of the creatures got her back up, and her paranoia that there could be one lurking close by.

"Are you all right?"

"I'm fine." Bronte patted the knitting pattern and tried to think of pleasant things. "So in a nutshell you want me to knit this hat-beard combo for your new boyfriend so he can bond better with his tutor?"

"Silly," Eileen whacked playfully at her arm. "It's for me."

"You?"

"Andy'll think it's right mad," she continued, oblivious to the look on Bronte's face. "Do you think you could run one up for me?"

Bronte felt old before her time. The longer she existed the less she understood people. "Sure. But you're buying the wool."

"Brilliant." She skipped back a few steps from the desk, mission accomplished. "I wouldn't know where to get it, could I just pay you back?"

"Yes."

"Better get back, only supposed to have a five minute loo stop." She started off down the centre of the shop in the direction of the diner before pausing to look back at Bronte. "I'm seeing him this Saturday," she added, casually and hopefully adding a deadline.

"I'll try my best," Bronte trilled after her as she skipped away. Checking the lay of the land for Lillian or any customers needing help, she pulled the magazine back out from under the paper bags and returned to the serious business of the day.

Arriving at home with a dripping bag of ice cream, Bronte realised that the banana spilt thing wasn't going to happen. In her kitchen she stood and surveyed the mess with scorn. It was an accepted fact that food didn't keep long in this kind of heat, but she hadn't expected things to disintegrate so quickly. The bunch of bananas she had bought yesterday had liquefied in the summer heat. The skins were blackening rapidly, and one of the bananas looked as though it had exploded, its pungent mushy flesh seeping out across the kitchen work top. A couple of flies that had been paddling in the sticky mash darted away at Bronte's intrusion and went to vibrate against the kitchen window.

"Brilliant, just brilliant," she muttered as she threw the ice cream into the freezer, kicking the door shut. Wrinkling her nose, she picked up the bananas by the neck and hurriedly deposited them into the bin. Running the dish cloth under the cold tap, she wiped up the leaking banana mush whilst the flies returned, bewildered at the disappearance of their lucky find.

In the living room another gang of flies were doing laps around the ceiling lamp. Bronte went up to the mirror and took her earrings out. She gazed down at the mantelpiece and a frown creased her brow as she noted that the dust had been disturbed. It looked as though a small feather duster had bounced its way down the length of the surface, leaving clear circles in the stretch of dust.

"What on earth?" She put a hand to the edge of the mantelpiece and a fly landed on the back of her hand. "Bloody flies!" she waved the insect off and it landed primly in the middle of the mirror before her. Too furious to think beyond the moment, she glared at the fly before slamming her hand palm down onto the mirror and killing the fly. "Hah!" she declared triumphantly although her smile dropped when she took her hand away and saw the insect guts on her skin.

She found suitable wool for Eileen's beard-hat in her own stash, and spent the evening in the humid atmosphere of her living room knitting a beard. She held it up when completed. She had to be mad knitting facial hair in these temperatures. Still, she'd get the hat made tomorrow and then it would be ready for the weekend and Eileen's seduction of the nerdy uni student.

As the evening drew on, she put her knitting needles away and tidied up a little around the house – Bronte's definition of "tidy" – and went to take the bin out. Out of the kitchen door she had a small walled yard, opening out onto a footpath alley where everyone kept their black wheelie bins. The yard walls were about shoulder height, and every house had a matching set. These were old houses for the mill workers in the 1800s, constructed by a benevolent owner who believed that happy workers who got to live in respectable conditions, would be more productive workers. It was an odd idea for a rich man to have, back in the times it was assumed people were only poor because they were either too drunk, stupid or bone idle to do anything about it.

Her next door neighbour, Albert, a retired man with a bald head and a scraggy neck, was perched out in his own back yard smoking a pipe and gazing wistfully up into the branches of the silver birch that took up most of the space in his small plot of land.

"Evening, lass," he nodded to her as she returned from the bin.

"Now then, Albert."

"Not needing any unwelcome guests removing?"

Bronte paused and watched the blue-grey smoke of burning tobacco twist up in the evening air. "No, wrong time of year." It had happened upon occasion that her spider scooper hadn't been able to get into a particular crevice where a spider had chosen to visibly sit and laugh at her. To say Bronte was scared of spiders was probably an understatement. She liked to think she was an adult, an independent woman who dealt with living alone quite well. But sometimes she had been forced by her own paralysing fear to go next door and fetch her elderly neighbour round to kill the spider before she'd be able to move freely again in her own home. It never ceased to amuse Albert when he was called upon for his hunting skills, making some comment that there had never been so much fuss when the old girl had been living here.

"Aye, well," he sighed, sucking on his pipe. "When autumn comes, you come knocking."

"Good night, Albert."

She locked the back door, then turned to the kitchen and shivered with that uncanny feeling that she was being watched. There was no one there but herself and a troop of half dozy flies. She went up to bed. It would soon be the start of another working day.

The weather broke on Sunday morning. Broiling and thickening clouds gathered across the sky, pulsating with moisture and energy. There was a brief stint of thunder and lightning, before a steady outpouring of rain settled across the day. Bronte gazed out of the front window as she half-listened to her mother ramble down the telephone.

It looked as though she wasn't going out today either. She had been housebound for the entire weekend, although mostly out of thoughtlessness and personal choice. She could lose days puttering around at home. For evenings out she needed external stimuli, usually in the form of Eileen, to get her moving. Eileen had been in Leeds over the weekend, testing out her new beard-hat on her student lover. As she told Bronte later in the week, it had caused some amusement, although when she had approached her man in the bedroom, still wearing it, she had been told in no uncertain terms to take it off. Bronte had given a little shudder. The scene barely warranted thinking about.

On Sunday morning she still knew nothing of this, and was hearing of the small incidences in her mother's existence. It was raining heavily in Skipton, where her parents lived, and her mother delighted in telling her all about the rain, as if such a thing had never been seen in Saltaire.

"And old peg-leg is moaning a bucket full because the rain makes his knee ache. The one he doesn't even have."

Peg-leg, Bronte's father, was a seventy-one year old ex hill farmer who had been forced out of the farming life after losing his right leg to a traffic accident. With the onset of age and his wife's niggling worries of isolated living, they had sold up the hill farm and moved to the outskirts of Skipton. Neither of their children had shown any inclination for farming, and as much as Bronte's father hadn't wanted to see the farm go out of the family, what else was there to be done? With the money left over once the farm was sold and the new property bought, they had talked of going on cruises and seeing the world, although little in that line had happened yet. A Yorkshire man and his money were not easily parted.

"It will be nice to sleep easier at nights," her mother continued. "This heat has been dreadful. And food just hasn't kept."

"I know," Bronte sighed, turning away from the window. "We've had a plague of flies over here. They're driving me nuts." As she said it, she looked to the lightshade where the little buggers liked to congregate, but realised there were none, in fact the living room appeared to be fly-free. Perhaps it was the sudden change in weather.

"Dirty creatures. I hope you've got fly paper up."

"Yeah, I got one of those spiral things, you know, death in a roll. There's hundreds of the things stuck on it now." Bronte wandered through into the kitchen with the cordless phone.

"Always used to get an influx of them when we cleaned the sheds out."

Bronte stared up at the ceiling, her brow creasing in mild confusion. How odd. The top half of the sticky fly roll was empty of insect corpses. Perhaps the glue had melted in the heat and slid down the roll, dragging the bodies with it. She went to look at the kitchen table to check for any drippings, but there was nothing there.

"...still, we endeavour to survive..."

"You heard from Branwell recently?" She interrupted, not having listened to a word her mother said for the past minute.

"Branwell, your brother?"

"He's the only Branwell I know."

"Oh, he was away to another interview. I haven't heard from him so I don't know how it went. Where was it he went?" She suddenly yelled, presumably at her husband somewhere in the house in Skipton. All the volume went directly down the telephone line and into Bronte's inner ear, making her wince.

"You say where now?"

"Mother, you don't have to shout," she muttered.

"Skye. That's the place. It's all the way up in bloody Scotland. I don't know why he wants to be going all the way up there. I'll never see him. And it's not like we don't have the birds here."

"You know Branwell: always itchy feet."

"He should have taken over the farm."

"He didn't want to be a sheep farmer."

Bronte's brother, Branwell, was a wildlife ranger who specialised in ornithology. He had worked his way up through various nature conservation jobs over the years. He was now capable of managing nature reserves and heading up special conservation projects for birds, the birds of prey family branch being particularly en vogue at present. He also suffered from what Bronte referred to as itchy feet, and every couple of years he was ready to move on and try living somewhere new. He relished the feeling of getting to know a new area, not as a tourist, but as a local. The feeling always wore off and his eyes would start the eternal search for new jobs. Nowhere had managed to hold him all that long. He'd lived all over Yorkshire, and had also been way down south to Wiltshire working in the chalk lands of ancient monuments and rolling plains of grassland. Clearly the high human population of the south of England was getting too much if he was looking for the real wildernesses of the UK and setting his sights on the highlands and islands of Scotland.

"Love, I'd better go," her mother said. "I need to get this joint sorted out for the Sunday roast, and modern cookers still confuse your father."

"Sure. I'll speak to you another day."

Bronte hung up and put the phone down on the kitchen table. She gazed back up at the fly paper in bewilderment. She was definitely missing some dead flies. Not that she was particularly possessive about her fly corpses, only that she knew from her slovenly domestic habits that dead flies could lay about for months.

Odd little incidences continued to occur. On Monday morning she took a mug from the mug tree and found short pieces of brown wool curled up in the bottom of the mug. They looked like leftovers from the beard-hat project from the previous week. I'm going mad, she thought, why would I leave wool in a cup? When she went into the living room to put her earrings on in front of the mirror, she noted that the mantelpiece had been completely dusted. She couldn't remember the last time she had seen it so clean, and had in fact forgotten that it had such a deep dark colour.

Perhaps she'd taken to sleepwalking, she mused, as she noted the time and realised she was going to be late if she didn't get a move on. In her subconscious frustration at the messy house, she had decided to clean in her sleep. Even if that meant illogical behaviour such as tidying wool away into cups.

Paul Warren was a clean-shaven, olive-skinned, bohemian in-fashion gent rather taken with modern fashions based on the clothing of nineteenth century farm workers. He was all waistcoats with matching trousers, boutique flat caps and the occasional cravat. Illustrated arms carried the best of tattoos. He was also a charismatic charmer who had wooed and bedded most of the women in the mill, baring Bronte, Lillian (as far as anyone knew) and old Mrs Gouthwaite of the doddery bladder who worked on the tourist information desk. He had worked his charm through a fair part of the town and neighbouring Shipley. If it wasn't for the fact that the population kept getting older and a new batch of of-age girls joined the legions of naive geese every year, he would have had to have moved on years ago in search of new conquests.

Bronte had neither a doddery bladder (Mrs Gouthwaite) nor extreme anger management issues (Lillian) and yet she had managed to resist the Warren offensive this long. It was down to a mixture of her own absent mindedness, slowness at picking up hints (he would tell her which pub he would be frequenting that evening – Bronte never appeared) and an old-fashioned and perhaps deluded idea of the sanctity of long-term relationships, meaningful connections and all that romantic dross. Which was rather ironic when one considered how long Bronte had been single. She didn't much like sharing either, and the fact that Paul was an easy slut was a tad off putting. Yet when one was talking to him, he had a knack of making you believe you were the most stunning and captivating creature on earth. You were the one that would take him away from the one night stands and meaningless flings. You were what he had been waiting for.

He worked in a small gentleman's outfitters that ought not to have had sufficient custom in such a small place, but thanks to the internet and trading off Saltaire's name, was able to make a respectable profit. On his lunch breaks Paul liked to wander the many establishments of town, networking and sizing up new potential victims. He was a regular at the mill, to gaze at the colourful works in the art gallery or indulge in cheerful banter with staff. And of course there were a few empty boxes on the tick list of mill women.

Bronte was leaning against the shop wall, watching the rain through one of the large draughty windows. She was tidying up a waste-of-space display that a mother's bunch of unruly children had knocked over. They should have smashed it up, she reflected, because no one in their right mind was going to buy these decorations. Who would spend seventy pounds on a small wooden tree to stand on their window sill? Only to spend another thirty to forty pounds on little wooden leaves and birds to hang in said tree? It was all sold, priced and packaged as artisan products, and perhaps if it had been locally made, covered in support-your-local-craftswomen stickers and oozing goodness and charm, it would have been worth it. Except this stuff was mass produced in China on big industrial computer-run ban saws, with underpaid workers snapping out the shapes and boxing up the decorations.

She'd found all of the mini hangers that had been knocked off the display trees, and piled them up on a neighbouring table displaying art books that hadn't sold for months. She was slowly untangling the string and wondering what she might cook for her dinner this evening.

"Now then, Bronte," Paul Warren, complete in Paisley shirt and grey woollen waistcoat, flat cap at a jaunty angle, twinkled into her personal space. "You all right? Bit of window dressing going on here?"

She smiled wanly. "Something like that. Thanks to our more enthusiastic customers."

"Did they buy anything after this?"

"Did they hell."

"They never do, do they?" he sighed. "I never thought I was going to get away on my break today. Couple of Spanish tourists, done the mill and wanted a bit of retail therapy. Wanted to try one every bloody thing in the shop. Didn't buy anything in the end."

"What, you couldn't charm them into one little thing?"

"I think you know better than anyone that my charm doesn't always work."

She chose to ignore the dig. She didn't mind him; in fact Paul was always very good for a chat when he homed in on you. It was just that whenever you then saw him chatting to someone else, you realised how superficial and meaningless it all was.

"Let me help you."

"Don't you get enough of tidying up after customers?"

"We don't have wooden birds back at the shop," he told her, picking up a few of the decorations to untangle the strings. He mirrored her position, leaning into the opposite side of the window sill. "We get a few coming in to buy stuff though."

Bronte gave a little laugh.

"I missed seeing you about town at the weekend," Paul changed the subject. He'd lined three of the birds to hang off his forefinger. "You go into Leeds, like?"

"I didn't go anywhere this weekend, just a quiet one."

"Quiet one!" Paul almost roared, "Bronte, lass, you're in the prime of your life. You want to be out there, doing and living. You're too good for being shut away."

"I'm not suffering. We'll have to see the next time Eileen drags me out."

"She wasn't out in town either."

"She was in Leeds."

"You didn't fancy that?"

"Wasn't invited." She caught his eye. "Eileen's got a new man. A university boy."

Paul didn't look too impressed. "We should go out. I've always fancied a night out with Eileen and Bronte. I never seem to manage to get anywhere with you."

"Mr Warren, are you here to buy something or are you just harassing my staff?" Lillian appeared, her eyes flashing in irritation.

"Aye up," Paul muttered under his breath, pushed his hat to a sensible angle on his head and straightened his posture. "Just asking about these decorations here. But I don't think wooden birds are my cup of tea." He slid the birds off his finger into Bronte's palm, and folded her fingers around them, taking his time with the contact.

"For God's sake, Paul," Lillian snapped. "Will you save your conquests for out-of-working hours?"

Paul gave her a cheeky grin. "Best be off, else I'll be late for the afternoon shift. Be seeing you, Bronte."

Lillian let out a sigh and watched the man saunter off down the bookshop to the stairwell. "Do you know he tried to seduce me over my desk once?"

Bronte's eyebrows bounced up for a fleeting second before she regained control of her demeanour.

"Of course, I would have thought you would have had more self respect. He's had more women than hot dinners." Lillian tapped a painted nail to her lips. "I turned him down. On *that* occasion."

Bronte couldn't help herself. "You've got better self restraint than Mrs Gouthwaite. I heard she flung an entire box of Halifax brochures to the floor when he turned up in her office."

Lillian looked horrified. From Bronte's deadpan expression, she was not entirely sure that it wasn't the truth. "He wouldn't..."

"I've got some books behind the desk to put out," Bronte said, evading the question. "Back to work."

The day it first happened Bronte was stretched lengthways on her beat up, sagging sofa. It was a weekday evening. Her bare feet rested on one arm, and at the other she had a jumble of cushions to prop herself up in a comfortable lounging position. With her back to the window, she was reading a paperback, with music playing to accompany the mood. The CD was starting the last track of the album when she happened to glance up at the painting on the back living room wall.

It was a large canvas painting she'd done years ago, supposedly an impressionist-style depiction of a breeze going through a wild grass meadow in summer. It hadn't quite worked out as she'd hoped, but the colours were nice and it brightened up a large space of cream painted plaster.

Yet it was not her art work she was specifically looking at.

In the first moment she did not realise why she had been alerted to the wall. There was that instinctual nervousness, a creeping dread running up her back and into her shoulders, that hadn't yet been translated by her consciousness as fear. With a first glance into a room, there is precious little we actually see. Instead great swathes are filled in by our memory, for our brain is too lazy to have to look at the same old tired objects every single time. And thus, there can be a moment when you know there is something out of place but you can not quite see it.

There was a small dark crack coming out from behind the left hand side of the canvas. It was only a few centimetres long but quite wide for a crack.

Bronte felt her fingers grow clammy.

The crack began to grow, extending in length from behind the canvas. It was at least ten centimetres now and still a single crack.

Her fingers locked into position around the paperback book. A horror clutched at her chest and she felt as though she was vacuum formed against the sofa. There was a thought in her head that she needed to get out of the room but she could not move.

The crack came out a little further, then a bend appeared in it. A second crack began to tentatively slip out from under the canvas, testing the air.

Everyone has a fear of something, some more irrational than others. When faced with it there is a paralysing moment of horror and disbelief that the nightmare object is materialising. Then the primeval reaction kicks in, whether that be to scream, run, sob or collapse into a shaking pile of nerves. The time between the first moment and the reaction is mere seconds but at the time it feels like a lifetime of torture.

The canvas gave a slight jolt as if there was something big behind it. Judging by the length of those cracks, it would have to be big.

Bronte knew they weren't cracks.

Her survival instinct kicked in. She bolted out of the sofa, whipping her legs up to her body and scrambling back over the arm rest furthest from the back wall. Her legs were shaking. She could not help herself. When the third crack started to slip out, she let out a shrill, high decibel scream and fled out of the first door she came to.

From the front door she stumbled over herself to get out of the building. She was shaking, and she could feel the start of tears pricking at her eyes. She ran for the front wall that enclosed the tiny garden in front of her terrace house, and leaned up against it. She stared back at her house in horror, knowing she would never be able to set foot in it again.

Bronte was an archnophobe. Even the smallest of spiders that the British Isles had to offer up would send her into a nervous panic. The inert spiders that dangled upside down waiting for dinner to stroll by made her feel ill. The giant house spiders that scuttled in during autumn to run across the carpet like demonic mice put her into a paralysing sweat. Given that her parents had never had a fear of bugs, and her brother Branwell was positively fascinated by any living creature, no one could really understand how she had developed such an irrational and deeply placed terror.

She had tried to get help with a hypnotherapist, and wasted a hundred pounds on a very ill-thought treatment that had only made things worse. The hypnotherapist hadn't put Bronte under properly, although they were both so desperate for it to work, both went along with pretending. Bronte had then woken up properly, lying on the vintage therapy couch. She had opened her eyes to see a full blown tarantula sitting on the hem of her skirt. The therapist had thought that when she woke up to find spiders crawling over her, and no harm having occurred, she'd realise the error of her ways and be cured. Instead Bronte had panicked and starting screaming. The woman in the waiting room with the next appointment had picked up her handbag and walked out. The tarantula had panicked and reared up as if to attack. Bronte had jumped up from the couch, shaking her skirts long after the creature had fallen off. She'd seen it on the floor, giving her a look as if it meant to chase her out of the room. She hadn't thought. She had grabbed at the first thing to hand, a heavy tome of a book, and lobbed it at the spider. The projectile hit its mark with a sickening crunch. The spider was no more. Bronte had grabbed her bag and run sobbing from the building, whilst the therapist stood in numb horror looking at what had happened. He tentatively lifted up the book and wondered what he was going to tell his friend about the loaned pet tarantula.

"God almighty lass, what's all't screaming about?"

The cyclical terror was broken. From the neighbouring front door Albert peered out into the evening. His face creased further in concern when he saw her shaking and sobbing. There were performances now and then about bugs in the house, but they hadn't had one on this level before.

"You had some bad news?"

She shook her head and pointed at the house.

"This is about a spider?"

"No."

"No?" He was pleasantly surprised for a moment. Perhaps they were making progress on the irrational spider fear.

"That wasn't a British spider. It was... a mutant."

"A mutant spider?"

"Tropical. Its legs..." she held her hands apart to demonstrate.

"There's no spiders as big as that," he scoffed. "You're imagining things."

"It's in there."

"Shall we go and sort it out then?"

"I'm not going back in that house."

"I think you'll have to at some point," Albert muttered, coming down the front steps and wandering around to Bronte's front yard. "Away now, let's go in and deal with this."

"I can't go in there."

"Yes you can," he said, not taking her protests all that seriously. He had been dozing off in the living to some boring programme on the television when Bronte's screams had whipped him out of his slumber. "You're going to have to get yourself a boyfriend, Bronte," he advised as he trotted in through the front door. "Either that or a trained cat. I can't be forever coming over to rescue you."

Bronte went to the front door and stood on the threshold, refusing to go any further. She could see the painting. The cracks had disappeared, probably swiftly withdrawn to the safety of the canvas when she'd started screaming. The CD she had been listening to had come to an end, and there was silence in the room. Or rather not silence, but that sound of someone holding their breath. Of watching eyes. Of pretending they weren't there, when everyone knew that they were.

Albert was in the middle of the living room, looking around. "So where is it?"

"It's massive. It's probably dangerous."

"Probably invisible."

She pointed. "It's behind that painting. But those legs were so long. It must have escaped from a zoo. It won't be safe..." She squeezed her eyes shut and held her curled up fingers to her mouth as Albert brashly went up to the wall and took down the painting. She couldn't watch.

"There's nothing there."

She tentatively started to open her eyes, and when she realised the wall was blank, she opened them fully. There was nothing on the wall, not even the slightest of cracks in the plastering. She looked to Albert holding the canvas. "It'll be on the back of the painting, oh god, you'd better drop it before it attacks..."

Albert spun the canvas around in nimble fingers. Bronte gave a little yelp at the suddenness of it. There was nothing hunkered down underneath the canvas, clinging on to the frame and hoping it wouldn't be seen. The painting was spider free.

Albert looked at her with pity. "There's nothing here."

She couldn't quite understand it. "I saw the legs."

"Maybe you were dreaming. I know I fell asleep in the chair this evening." He hooked the canvas back onto the single nail sticking out of the wall. "You've got to get help; you can't carry on like this, can you?"

"It was definitely there."

"There's nothing here," Albert repeated. "Screaming about real spiders is one thing, but letting imaginary mutant spiders chase you out of your own house is an altogether different kettle of fish."

"I don't understand it."

He sighed. "It's late, and you'll have work in the morning, won't you? Go to bed and sleep it off. You'll realise it was all in your head in the morning. But you want to be talking to your doctor about this. Good night."

He closed the front door behind him as he left, Bronte murmuring thanks and apologies for the disturbance. She was alone in her silent living room. She locked the front door then turned to survey the room. There was nothing there. Yet she had that horrible sensation of being watched.

She bolted upstairs, hurriedly completed her ablutions in the bathroom, then ran into the bedroom. Rolling up a towel, she pushed it against the bottom of the door to be sure that nothing would be able to creep in during the night. She jumped into bed and hid under the duvet, shaking and thinking that she would never be able to go downstairs again.

Despite the previous evening's drama life continued. Waking up the following morning and creeping downstairs, Bronte felt rather foolish to think of all the noise and fuss she had created. Spiders simply weren't that large. Either it had been her imagination, or the evening shadows had elongated and created an illusion on the back wall. It was the wrong time of year even for the English spiders to be causing trouble.

In the kitchen she sat drinking tea and staring at the fly paper that was now completely clear of dead flies. Had the glue lost its potency and the flies had managed to wriggle free? Not possible, she thought, for even if they had fallen off, they still would have been dead.

You need to get a grip, she told herself. People are going to start thinking you're having a nervous breakdown. And it wasn't even as though she was suffering a great personal trauma, unless the regularity of life could be classed as such a thing. Swilling her mug out, she left it in the sink and headed for work.

Work dragged itself through the day. Eileen wasn't in as she'd booked a couple of days off to recover from a festival. There seemed to be more tourists than usual in the mill, wandering around asking stupid questions and not understanding how to get to the next floor. Bronte had a sense of unease that she continued to repress. There was nothing to worry about. There was nothing waiting for her at home.

After work she trudged up the hill to get to the main road where modern architecture had attached itself to the Victorian finery of the village. Here there were modern shops, real life and local amenities. On the way up she passed the line of shops in the old village. She walked past the gentleman's outfitters where Paul worked, as she always did when she was going up the hill. Paul hung out of the front door, tipping his flat cap to her.

"Afternoon Bronte, looking ravishing as always."

"Paul," she nodded to him, not slowing her pace.

"There a fire somewhere?"

She smiled to herself but didn't stop. "I'm hungry," she called over her shoulder. "Got to get myself to the shops."

"You inviting me over for supper?"

"Didn't sound like it." Christ, he was desperate, she told herself whilst trying to stop the smile from spreading too far across her face. It wasn't like she was anything special, and he could and did have any woman he liked.

She got a few groceries in, had a good pick over the reduced bread shelf and got a couple of bits for the freezer. She decided to walk back down the side streets and around to George Street, where she lived, so as to avoid going back past Paul's place of work.

She returned home in high spirits, little knowing that this evening was to be one of the trigger points in her life. One of those life-defining, life-changing moments upon which the entire future so precariously hinged. Although at the time it would never seem to be so intensely important. She unlocked the front door and wandered through to the kitchen, kicking off her shoes on the way. She got the water on the boil on the hob top for pasta, put the bread in the freezer, then washed off a couple of peppers under the cold tap. She put the wooden chopping board on the table with the peppers lined up for execution. Turning back to the worktop, she took a knife from the knife block and returned to her peppers.

That was the moment. Bronte gagged on a gasp and staggered backwards, dropping the knife and hitting the small of her back against the sink. The knife blade stabbed down into the lino, missing her toes by millimetres. Her eyes blinked and tried to refocus, a small sliver of rational brain telling her this simply wasn't possible. It had to be a trick or an illusion or a hallucination. Her pulse went up and her eyes started to fill in terror.

In the middle of the table stood a spider.

It was the biggest spider Bronte had ever seen in her life. This was by no means an exaggeration of the traumatised archnophobe, nor a statement on the evolution of the English house spider. This was in fact the biggest spider anyone had ever seen. Anyone in the entire world. It was the biggest spider that had ever been. And it was standing on Bronte's kitchen table.

This is not to suggest there was a spider the size of an Alsatian sitting on the table, for such an idea would be nonsense. As far as leg span went, it would have been marginally larger than the biggest huntsman or goliath bird eating tarantula recorded, but an inch here or there wouldn't have been particularly note worthy if one was faced with two massive spiders on a table. To say they were about a foot in length toe-to-toe, thirty centimetres for the metric generation, would capture the general spirit of the thing. The body was massive, and far more bulbous than a regular spider. In fact it was as though a couple of bloated balls had been pushed together. Added to that was the hair. This was a hairy beast. Not on a hairy tarantula level, but ramped up so that it resembled something of a dark haired pom-pom. What Bronte didn't appreciate or care about just at the particular moment was that this spider was a mutated freak. Usually mutations happened slowly in nature over many generations, but for this spider much had happened all at once. Had it been in its natural home in the jungle, it would have been shunned by the other spiders for being just too freakish. No one was meant to have that many hairs per square inch, and the hairs definitely weren't meant to be that long. And as for that over inflated fat body, don't let those South American spiders even get started on that subject. For this was a South American spider and a stowaway who had come to the UK in a crate of bananas. It had eaten its way through most of the bananas and hollowed out a hiding place in one of the few intact bunches when it realised people were coming. A lot of the crate's contents had been thrown out, a couple of bunches rescued and put on a pallet destined for Yorkshire. The rest, as they say, was history.

Bronte could feel her very flesh trying to melt and spread itself out against the kitchen worktop, hoping it could then crawl across the kitchen sink and out of the window. "It's just your imagination," she whispered. Perhaps it was an insane knitting project she had done in her sleep.

The spider tentatively moved one of its long legs to the side. Bronte let out a squeal and put her hand to her mouth. It wasn't a knitting project. It was alive. The damn thing was alive. In saner moments she might have congratulated herself that she hadn't screamed or passed out. But she was unable to move her legs. Her hand started to slide across to the draining board. She could feel her heart hammering in her chest as if it wanted to break free of her ribcage. There was no one to help her. She was all alone. She was going to have to kill this thing on her own. Then she'd run screaming to Albert and get him to clean up the mess. But she couldn't run yet, because that thing was watching her and it would go for her if she tried to nip out the back door. Her fingers touched the handle of the frying pan. Thank Christ she had found something up to the job.

The old saying intended to help children overcome their fear of spiders was partially true in this case. You're not scared of that little thing are you? It's more scared of you than you are of it. Although Bronte was sure it was staring at her, the eyes somehow blended in with all that thick dark hair. The fact was that the spider wasn't looking at anything for it had its eyes closed.

Her fingers tightened around the frying pan handle. Her nostrils flared in determination. She was terrified but she had to do this. She was an independent woman. She was going to win. As her arm muscles tensed in readiness to bring the frying pan smashing down onto the kitchen table, a strange thing happened. The spider opened its eyes and looked at her. And as strange a turn of events as it was, it was this that saved its life.

This spider was a freak. The large body and the long and tightly packed hair gave it the look of an obese pom pom rather than a tarantula. Its legs were longer than the usual tarantula, as though its mother had once had a dalliance with an Australian huntsman. Whether taking the size from body or leg span, either way it was the biggest spider ever witnessed. But the biggest mutation was the eyes.

With non web spinning spiders, that would be said the hunting ones that did the running and the jumping, eight frontal eyes were normal. There would be two larger eyes, with three smaller eyes to each side. All the better to see you with, my dear. In this spider, the ocular functions had been intensified and changed in very odd ways, even for the bizarrely formed insect and arachnid world. This spider only had six eyes to start with, four of which were of average minor eye-size, sitting on each side of the main eyes. The main eyes were massive for a spider, round and with a bluish tinge. Such big eyes could dry out, so nature had decreed in this case eyelids of a reptilian variety would be of use, and added dark lids. Not only was this the biggest spider ever seen, but it was the first one ever blessed with the ability to close its eyes.

So when Bronte had thought it had been watching her, she had actually seen the dark eyelids. Who had been more frightened was never to be quantified. And when the spider opened its eyes, she saw two bright buttons staring up at her. She was almost sure she saw herself reflected. It was this unexpected occurrence that made her falter and let go of the frying pan.

The spider had a rather mournful look about it, as if it were about to start sobbing. How could anyone think to mash it into the kitchen tablecloth with a frying pan? It slowly walked backwards as if getting some distance from the lunatic. The very movement of a spider's eight legs made her stomach turn, but she was unable to attack now. The spider paused, then made a neat leap across to the far worktop and made for the mug tree.

"What the hell?"

She kept her back pressed to the cupboards, but moved around to get a better view of her mug tree. And there it was, reversed into the mug, its body completely filling the tea receptacle, resting on a bed of woollen strands, and its feet dangling out of the mug. The spider blinked and watched her from its ceramic cave.

She raised a hand as if to point at it and tell it what for, before her brain clicked in and she returned to type. There was a spider in the house and she had to get out.

Flicking the catch back, she wrenched open the kitchen door and fled out into the back yard. Scrambling over the joining wall, she tumbled into Albert's garden and started hammering on the kitchen door.

"Who the bloody hell is that!" An irate voice yelled from the living room. "Don't you know folk are eating their tea now?"

Bronte continued to pound her fists on the door.

Accompanied by grumbling and swearing, the lock clicked and the door opened. Albert met with a dishevelled Bronte wobbling at the door and out of breath as if she'd just run a marathon.

"What the hell's happened to you?"

She pointed at her home. "It's back."

"What?"

"Last night."

"Last night?" Realisation dawned on his face. "You've interrupted my tea for a bloody spider? Bronte, this has got to stop. You need help, lass."

"It's not just any spider," she coughed. "It's the biggest spider ever."

"Yeah, and I've not heard that one before." He let out a long sigh. "I'm not usually one to press people into pills, but I think you need to see someone about this."

"I'm not making this up. You come and see."

"All right."

They took the more sedate route of going out of the gate into the back alley, then through Bronte's own yard and into the kitchen.

"Where is it then?"

"In the mug on the mug tree. The big one with the sea view painted on it."

Albert walked up to the mug tree and unhooked the offending mug. "This?" he asked, turning to her and holding up the offending mug. "There's nowt in here but a few scraggy pieces of wool."

"It must be in another mug."

He spun the mug tree around. "There's nowt here."

"But..."

"There's nowt here, and I don't think there ever was." He put the mug down on the kitchen table. "What's really bothering you?"

"Nothing. I'm not making this up."

"You had a holiday recently?"

"No, but that's not the point..."

"I think you should take a break from this place; go up to Skipton and see your folks for a bit. And maybe think about seeing someone. Nip it in the bud whilst you still can." He patted her shoulder as he headed back out the kitchen door. "I'm missing my programme, you'll excuse me now."

Bronte stood forlornly in the middle of the room and looked around her spider free kitchen. She was sure of what she had seen. It couldn't possibly have been her imagination.

There had been no spider in the kitchen the following morning. A brief examination of the mug tree had shown those strands of wool still to be in place, but that was all. Random wool was no proof of giant spiders. She was going mad.

Instead of painting before work, she had gone online and ordered train tickets. She was free the next couple of days as she was working the coming weekend. She would take Albert's advice and get away. Nip it in the bud. Being terrified over spiders was bad enough, but imaginary spiders? She packed up what she thought she would need for a few days in a small bag, and went to work. She'd get the train to Skipton straight after her shift and have a change of scene.

In the afternoon she told Eileen of what had been going on.

Eileen rolled her eyes. "You definitely need to shake things up a bit if you're seeing spiders, Bronte. I worry about you spending too much time on your own. What you need is a man."

"For God's sake, Eileen. Sex isn't the solution to everything."

She jiggled her shoulders. "I wouldn't judge till you've tried it."

Bronte scowled at her. "I have had sex before now, thank you."

"You know what I mean. You've been single a while. What are you saving yourself for? Live a bit and stop living in your head too much. Then that giant spider will just bugger off."

"I guess."

"You'll be back for the weekend though won't you?"

"Yeah, I'm working all weekend." Bronte paused, noted that Eileen was still looking expectantly at her. "That wasn't a casual question was it?"

"I'm just interested. Well, no, I want you to come out with us. They're having their monthly faculty dinner. It'll be a smaller occasion what with it being the summer. But some of them are back in Leeds this Saturday even though the next semester isn't starting for a good few weeks..."

"You're talking about your bug boy?"

"He's called Andy."

"I don't see how this is my problem."

"Those of them that have girlfriends or boyfriends sometimes bring them. I got to go to the last one and it was a right laugh. I mean, most of them are boffins, but they're bonkers. I was telling them about the Italian on the high street, so they're all getting the train over from Leeds on Saturday and we're going out for dinner. It's after the mill's shut..."

"You're not wanting me there?"

"Oh, come on, it'll be a laugh."

"Hanging out with people who have made bugs their lives?" Bronte sounded horrified. "Besides which, I don't know anyone..."

"There's this guy..."

"I don't like how this is starting."

"He's come over from Germany or Denmark or somewhere to do his PhD. He's only been here a couple of weeks, and he's single, so it would be good."

"I don't do blind dates."

"It's a big dinner; you just have to sit next to him. Come on, he's really nice. His name is Horst." Eileen fluttered her eyelashes. "I've not betrothed you to him. It doesn't have to be anything more than coming out and chatting to some weirdoes for a few hours."

"If you put it like that," Bronte muttered sarcastically.

"Brilliant. I'll text Andy and let him know. We're going to have such fun. You'll love it."

What the hell was she agreeing to, Bronte wondered as she waited on the platform for the Skipton train. If she was hallucinating giant spiders, it didn't seem like such a clever idea to agree to a dinner with a bunch of insect academics. No doubt they'd all be guffawing over their bug horror stories and at the very least she'd have nightmares. Either that or she'd go home that night and find a whole bloody tribe of woolly spiders living in the kitchen.

The railway went through the edge of Saltaire between the town and the mill, through its own dug out grove of train tracks crossing against the hill. The small, unmanned station was set down lower than the surrounding streets, each platform reached by its individual descending footpath. There were tubs of flowers along the far line of the platform, and a sturdy stone shelter with Victorian style wooden trim on either side.

Bronte watched the opposite platform where a collection of commuters and tourists waited for the train back to Leeds. The rails between them began to hiss and shriek to announce the incoming Skipton train. Bronte picked up her bag as the two-carriage train arrived. A handful of people got off, and Bronte and an overweight, hairy student firmly plugged into his headphones boarded the train.

Her father picked her up at the station in Skipton. His disability adapted car waited close to the front entrance in a disabled space. Despite the fact that he only had one leg, he didn't think of himself as disabled and would usually stubbornly park as far away as he could, just to prove that his prosthetic leg did the job just as well. But it was a busy pick up time at the station and nearing the hour he usually ate so he was keen to get home. Needs must sometimes.

"Thanks for fetching me."

Bronte had barely shut the passenger door before he was reversing the car out of the parking space. She pulled her seatbelt on, slipping her bag into the foot well. "I'm sure the world wouldn't end if you were a bit late for your dinner."

"Aye, you tell that to my stomach."

She suppressed a smile. There was nothing like an old farmer stuck in his ways. She leant her head against the window and watched the town as they passed by the little hospital and down to the small housing estate where her parents lived.

"It's a very sudden visit."

"I have a couple of days off work. I've got the weekend shift."

"Even so. Not in any trouble are you?"

"What?" She looked at him, a little aghast by the great leaps his mind was taking. "I've just come to see the two of you. There's no disaster coming."

"Not pregnant then?"

"No!"

"Well, you're of an age."

He parked up at the drive, Bronte's answers obviously satisfactory as the worried father chapter was pulled to an abrupt close. A retired sheepdog jumped up from his slumbering place on the doorstep, gave Bronte a woof in greeting before following Master into the house. After dinner and an old man's half hour for both of them, man and dog went out for an evening walk.

"He's got one of those springy blade things," her mother said as she passed her daughter a cup of tea. They were sitting on a stone bench in the back garden. "You know, like those paralympic runners use. He can go for miles on it, walking and walking. The dog's struggling to keep up with him. He even pinched it and hid it under the sofa one night."

"That bad?" Bronte wrapped her fingers around the mug. Even in summer, there was something about tea in the evening.

"Well, yes. He soon found it though. He's determined to prove there's nothing wrong with him."

"You'll have to get Sheppie a set of roller skates. He might be able to keep up then."

Her mother laughed and took a sip of tea. "Aye, and that won't raise eyebrows round here. Peg leg Seth and his rolling dog."

The two women settled into silence and watched the swallows perform their aeronautical acts across the sky.

"Have I always been scared of spiders?"

"What an odd question to ask." Emily looked at Bronte in consternation.

She shrugged. "Just curious; pondering on stupid things," she said, trying to make it more insignificant than it was. "I just wondered if I'd always been scared or if something happened to trigger it."

"You didn't have any traumatic childhood experiences if that's what you're getting at. I think the traumatic event was that hypnotherapist fleecing you of all that money..."

"Mother..."

"Well, I did think it was a waste of time even before you went. And then him trying to make you pay for that tarantula you killed. It wasn't your fault. Bloody idiot. You don't put giant spiders on sleeping folk who are terrified of them, and then wake them up. He ought to be sued for malpractice."

Bronte let out a long sigh. She'd had enough lectures on the wasted money, and enough comments about new fangled ideas that wouldn't work. She didn't suppose she was going to get the answer, whatever the question ought to be, to solve her imaginary spider problem.

"Did I tell you Branwell got that job?"

"No. It was only an interview last you mentioned it."

"He got it. He's moving to Skye at the end of the month. Lord but it's a long way."

"It'll be an adventure," Bronte said, feeling a little regretful. Branwell was never going to get rich, he simply wasn't in the right sector for money, but he was certainly going to live an interesting life. "Do you think I need to get myself sorted? Like a proper job and things?"

"A proper job?" Her mother, Emily, made it sound like a preposterous idea. "Isn't the one you've got now a proper job?"

"Well, yes of course it is." She ran a finger around the rim of her mug. "I meant more like a career. Something more demanding than standing around in a shop all day."

"What are you wanting to do?"

"I don't know," she sighed. The truth was she had no particular ambition for money or career or goals or plans or achievements. Yet with the appearance of the imagined spider, and comments from friends, she had started to worry that there was something missing from her life. That she had let herself grow stagnant. "Just so there's a point to my life."

Emily studied her daughter's profile for a moment or two before speaking. They had wondered if something was going on when she had phoned earlier in the day to tell them she was coming to visit for a couple of days. "I do feel sorry for you young folks these days," she started. "There's so much pressure for everyone to be achieving all the time. And it feels like everyone is expected to be very driven, to all want great careers. There's more than one way to have a fulfilling life. You have your art, Branwell has his birds..."

"Yeah, but it's not like I make any money with my art. At least Branwell's getting to travel about with his work."

"Is this about money? You're not in debt are you?"

"No," Bronte squeezed her eyes shut and placed a couple of fingers to the top of her nose. This was coming out wrong, all in all because she wasn't sure exactly what the problem was. "It's just some things that have happened recently..." she shuddered as a mental image of that giant spider flashed up. An expectant pom pom on legs with blue marbles for eyes. "Things people have said. It's started me thinking. Like I'm stagnant. I've been in Saltaire in four years in that house. Painting pictures no one sees, hanging around in a shop. Before I know it I'll be forty and I'll have done nothing."

"You're only thirty-one!"

"Eileen thinks I need a man."

"Maybe you do."

"Mother!"

Emily finished her tea. "I'm not saying you need to be a kept woman or have a man about to keep an eye on the little lady. I just worry you might get lonely rattling about on your own all the time. I mean it in the sense of companionship. I don't know, maybe you've gone off men and want a girlfriend."

"Don't start trying to be uber PC now. I'm having some type of existential crisis."

"You're lonely."

"I might have seen something."

"You're not on drugs are you?"

"Agghhhh." She balled her fingers up in frustration. Picked her mug up from the ground and stood up. "I shouldn't have started this; you're getting the wrong end of the stick."

"I hear of these art students. Having to get off their faces on drugs to find inspiration." Her mother's tone was getting shrill, like a disapproving maiden aunt.

"I'm not on drugs." Bronte closed the conversation. "I'm going in to see if there's anything on telly."

The next day Bronte wandered along the canal into town with her mother. They separated with Emily heading to the shops and Bronte wandering up to the castle with a sketchbook. She sat in a corner of the central courtyard and gazed up at the coiling yew tree in the middle of a ring of stone benches. It was hundreds of years old, and would probably still be here long after Bronte was dead. She gazed up into its branches, savouring the feeling of dappled sunlight filtering through the tumbled network of twigs. She needed to get out of the house more; that was all that the problem was. Beyond that, questions of careers, money and how many boyfriends you had were small potatoes. She was a dot on the earth, gone in the blink of an eye. None of this was worth seeing imaginary spiders for. She should go home, get back to work. The spider would be gone.

Bronte picked up the post from the doormat as she returned home one evening. Walking into the living room she dropped her bags onto the settee, giving the room a cursory glance. There were no spiders the size of rats. Her mind had calmed, and the change of scene had done her good. She ambled down to the kitchen, flicking through the collection of envelopes whilst trying to decide whether any of them would be worth opening.

She reached the kitchen sink, stopped and felt a hiss of terror reach back into her throat. Her feet were planted to the floor, yet her body tried to lean back as far as it would go. Her fingers tightened around the letters. There was a spider in the sink and her instinctive flight mixed with frozen terror reaction was kicking in. Yet she felt joy. This was a normal spider. Yes, it was one of those revolting fat-bodied house spiders one usually saw scuttling across the carpet on an evening in autumn to disappear behind a cupboard where you knew it sat, ever watching and waiting. But this wasn't imaginary, and no sensible person would react against it as though such a thing ought not to be seen in England.

Bronte considered running for Albert, but then after the previous episode, he probably would be less than enthusiastic about rescuing her. Perhaps now was the time to conquer this fear. She could fetch her spider scooper from the cupboard, be brave...

Bronte let out a little scream as a brown fuzzy ball lobbed itself into her sphere of vision, and landed with a dull thunk in the sink. The house spider pulled its legs together as if to try and look bigger than it was. Perhaps scare away the predator. It wasn't fooling anyone. After a moment it realised that wasn't going to work, and as all spiders are particularly well designed, it legged it. It didn't get very far before the particularly large and hairy spider caught up with it. Reaching out with disturbingly long legs, it snatched up the house spider and neatly rolled it up as if tying a parcel with its own limbs. Bringing it into its spidery embrace, it bit the prey, and the smaller spider stopped struggling.

The spider paused in its work and shifted to look directly at Bronte. It seemed to gaze up at her apologetically with its big blue eyes, as if to ask if she laid claim to this juicy morsel, having technically seen it first.

"You are not really here," Bronte said in a small voice.

The spider seemed to shrug to itself, and started wrapping its prey in silk.

She watched it for a few moments in horror. She didn't know if she was more horrified by the fact that there was a giant pom-pom spider in her sink, or the fact that her hallucinations were back. Surely this was too realistic to be a hallucination. Perhaps it was real. Perhaps it had escaped from the zoo. Or more bizarrely it could be someone's escaped pet. Why someone would want a spider as a house pet was beyond her.

What did people do when they found exotic escaped pets, or nasty pests in their house? The council? Or perhaps the RSPCA? Maybe they would want to come and collect it. She backed away into the living room and got her phone out of her bag. Finding the local animal sanctuary on the internet, she called the office.

"Hi, yes, do you keep a list of escaped pets?"

"Excuse me?"

"If someone's pet has escaped do you keep a list; I mean, in case it turns up somewhere?"

"Has your dog or cat gone missing?" the woman on the line asked. "You should have had them chipped, it's a legal requirement you know. When they turn up, we can scan them..."

Bronte crept up to the kitchen doorway and looked at the sink. She could see the top of the spider bobbing up and down in its work. "It's not a cat."

"A dog?"

"Something more exotic."

"Sorry?" The woman was starting to sound irritated. "Look, have you lost a pet or found something?"

"Do you have a list of lost pets in the area? Things like snakes and..."

"Have you found a snake in your house? You need to get an inspector round there right now. Don't try and handle it yourself."

An inspector. What would they think when they came to the house and found Bronte jabbering over something that was not in the sink? Something that did not exist. They'd call social services and she'd be locked up. Forced onto pills. Tied up in a straight jacket and thrown in a hole. Admittedly Bronte knew nothing about modern mental health practices but she didn't want officials coming into her home to point out that she was seeing things.

"Never mind," she told the woman. "I was just wondering."

"Just wondering? What do..."

Bronte hung up and turned her phone off in case the woman thought to redial. Very carefully, as if the floor was unstable, she slowly paced back into the kitchen and stopped by the table.

The spider climbed rather elegantly out of the sink, carrying a freshly wrapped parcel and stopped on the draining board. The arachnid and the archnophobe regarded one another.

"You are just a figment of my imagination."

The spider said nothing.

She'd heard about kids having imaginary friends, but this was beyond ridiculous. An imaginary spider. How was she supposed to deal with this? Just go with the flow until her brain worked out whatever problem she was trying to deal with? Then the spider would disappear on its own accord?

"I suppose I ought to give you a name," she said, trying to be brave and finding the only thing that occurred to her. She glanced around the kitchen, looking for inspiration, before her eyes dropped to the letters she was still carrying around with her. Bronte lived on George Street in Saltaire. She looked back at the spider. "George."

George blinked once, then ambled up onto the window sill in front of the sink. Reaching up with a couple of legs, he tapped at the glass in a random, jazz-like pattern. After a few bars, he stopped, shifting in position to look pleadingly at Bronte, before returning to tap out an unknown code on the glass.

Bronte looked in disbelief at the creature. "You want to be let out?"

She took a few steps towards the window without thinking, before stopping in a cold sweat. Unlatching the window and opening it would mean putting her hand and arm very close to where George was standing. What if it went for her, tried to bite her wrist? Was it even poisonous? It's a bloody imaginary spider, she scolded herself. It can't hurt you. But George looked so very real and her fear was instinctual. Even pictures of spiders could get the hairs on the back of her neck leaping up, and pictures were nothing more than arrangements of colour on paper.

George gave the window one forlorn tap.

"You'd better not try anything." She tried to sound like she meant business.

George politely took a few steps back from the window sill.

I cannot believe what I am doing, Bronte thought. Standing by the worktop she reached over and took hold of the window latch. It's not real, she repeated as a mantra in her head. That giant hairy tarantula standing by the taps isn't really there.

The frame creaked as the window opened. A burst of fresh air drifted inside. Bronte snatched her hand back as George gleefully went for the opening and scuttled out of the house, disappearing into the yard.

Bronte was alone. Breathless, she hung in the kitchen. Had it been that simple? Open the window and let your horrors out? Did this mean that she was cured now? She reached out and pulled the window a little closer so that it was only open a couple of notches. She fixed the window in position, then let her breath go. She had done it. She had faced her fear and let it out.

Things are never that simple.

Naturally George didn't wander off into the sunset, out of Bronte's worried mind never to be seen again. Since stepping forth from his banana beginnings, the only environment he had known was the terrace house on George Street. Once he had tended his larder and completed a little outdoor hunting, he slipped back into the house through an open window and squeezed his body into the oversized mug on the mug tree to rest.

The following morning Bronte got possibly the worst fright of her life whilst in the bathroom. She was in the shower, and had just turned around to let the hot water sluice the suds of shower gel from her back. At the exact same moment George decided to come off the ceiling and down the white tiles. He was a large, dark alien movement through the steam, unnatural in the mammal world with those fluidly moving eight legs. Bronte let out an involuntary ear-shattering scream as the giant spider moved down beside her. She slipped with surprise and grabbed onto the shower curtain rail to stop herself falling right over onto her backside. The shrill vibrations through the air were more than disturbing to George who reversed back across the tiled walls to the sink, all the time watching her with those big blue eyes for signs of threatening behaviour. The jury was still out as to whether this lumbering creature was of any danger to him.

The focus of those large eyes was beyond uncomfortable in this setting, and Bronte grabbed for a towel whilst the shower was still running on full power, just to cover her nakedness. The two being of completely different genus in the animal kingdom meant that the nakedness and body form of a human was utterly incomprehensible to a spider's mind, and certainly held no interest, sexual, perverse or otherwise. Not that logic had a lot to do in such impulsive circumstances.

"Get the hell out of the bathroom!" Bronte roared. "If I'm in here, you're not."

The door was shut and George was simply too large to shimmy under the crack between door and carpet as he'd just seen a native house spider do. He scuttled down behind the sink and out of sight. Now that the poorly tended larder of flies had been picked clean in the kitchen, and the house spiders were either dead or learning quickly this was not a house to inhabit; there was mainly only the army of woodlice that lived beneath the carpets that George could take. He would patrol the house every day, but found that outdoor hunting was a necessity to find enough sustenance. He would sometimes try other food items, and was known to suck a few grapes dry, leaving strange wrinkled little husks in the fruit bowl for Bronte to puzzle over.

Bronte wiped water from her eyes and looked around the bathroom whilst clutching the sodden towel uselessly to her chest. The spider seemed to have disappeared. She took a moment, waiting for her heart beat to slow down. She remained dripping until she felt she had enough control over her limbs to step out of the bath without slipping over.

"Jesus Christ," she swore to herself. She looked miserably at the drenched towel, before letting it drop into the bath. Grabbing a second towel, she quickly dried herself off and hurried out of the bathroom. She didn't close the door properly and George took his chance to sprint across the bathroom floor, out over the landing and into the spare bedroom. Bronte found him later on the window sill, furiously rubbing his body into the layers of dust that had built up. She watched for a minute or so in utter bewilderment as the great tarantula essentially dusted and polished the window sill. What did it think it was doing? At least it explained why her house was looking more dust free than it had done in years although it didn't make sense. She'd always thought spiders flourished in untidy and undusted houses where webs were allowed to hang indefinitely in corners.

She didn't have time to puzzle out the spider's behaviour. She had to get to work.

And so they settled into odd patterns of co existence, cautiously moving around one another with that lack of complete confidence that the other could not quite be trusted to not attempt an assassination at some point. Bronte would open the kitchen window in the way many people would to let the cat out. George would go out to explore the surrounding streets, becoming a terror to local mouse and rat populations, whilst at the same time unsettling neighbouring cats. They could tell that a new hunter had joined their domesticated territory, but they could not quite decide what to make of it. Most had enough sense to sniff in George's direction but keep a modest distance. A couple of cocky cats, the dominant felines on the street, went up to George with protruding claws on a dashed out paw to try and toy with the creature. George would soon rear up in attack poise, front legs waving and jaws mincing. Either the cat was sensible enough to back away or, in the confusion George would take his chance to run off, a brown hairy streak racing across the cobbled street beside the train tracks, and up the back alley to home.

When Bronte got home from work, she'd turn on music in the living room. One day she did so when George happened to be resting on top of one of the speakers. The sound waves vibrated up his leg hairs and into the thick jungle of overgrown body hair. He seemed to pulse with the gentle melody of chilled out acoustic guitar. Bronte watched in curiosity, then deciding to experiment a little, got a heavy rock album out and put it into the player. The volume and the almost hypnotic flurry of the drums, along with the deep bass thrumming, seemed to do odd things to the spider. To Bronte's eyes he seemed to start to dance, rearing his backside higher in the air and shaking it in time to the music. It wasn't head banging, but it was certainly something.

That Saturday when Bronte returned home from her weekend shift, all she felt like doing was lying prostrate on her settee like a zombie and watching a film. But in an hour Eileen would be coming to walk up to the restaurant with her for this damned dinner of bug men that Bronte was severely regretting she had agreed to. She didn't know anyone but Eileen, who would undoubtedly be fawning over the current boyfriend. Bronte was tired, and really not in the mood to have to listen to grown men enthuse over slugs, earwigs and whatever the hell else it was that they had decided to dedicate their studies to.

She left George sorting through an unravelled ball of wool that had fallen out of her stash bag yesterday evening. The big blue-eyed oversized tarantula ever so carefully shifted strands of wool about on the carpet. The eight legs were all moving in different directions, as it to arrange the wool in a complicated pattern. It was surreal. But then this was a product of her imagination, who said it had to make sense?

Bronte went upstairs, had a quick shower then sat on the end of her bed whilst blow drying her hair and wondering what on earth she was supposed to wear for a dinner with bug academics. Somehow she imagined them all in loose hiking gear, either that or geeky T-shirts and large spectacles. All a product of her own ignorance. But she didn't know what else to think and how on earth she was supposed to fit in. Fit in? She laughed at her own ridiculous thought. She was a self confessed archnophobe with an imaginary giant spider for an imaginary friend. She wasn't going to fit in. She may as well just be herself.

She changed her nose piercing to a bright shiny diamond, and added long dangly earrings. She tied her hair up loosely, intending to use a couple of Burmese hair sticks, but she could only find one, and absent-mindedly grabbed a short paintbrush as a substitute. She took a short sleeved emerald green silk dress out of the back of her wardrobe and added slender flip flops to the ensemble so that she wouldn't look too much like she was dressing up. Although Bronte had never been what she called the paranoid-single (people who needed to be constantly partnered up, for being stuck with themselves for any amount of time equated to torture), she had been wondering about this PhD student Eileen had mentioned. The student that was possibly from Denmark or Germany but probably wasn't from either. European. Not from round here. Perhaps she'd have a better chance with someone who didn't know what was classed as odd in the UK. Maybe Eileen was right when she said Bronte needed to shake things up a bit.

"You look nice," Eileen barely glanced at her as she typed something into her phone, jabbing away at the screen with her fingers.

"You do too," Bronte returned the compliment as she locked the front door.

The two women started to walk towards the main road, following an idle zig zag path up through the backstreets of Saltaire. They went past the little residential side alleys, and the community garden where the public bath house had been once upon a time. In philanthropic days when Titus Salt had been building and planning his little community of workers.

"So what was this guy's name?"

Eileen broke out into a grin as she put her phone in her handbag. "Oh, Bronte!" she nudged her friend with her elbow. "Are you waking up now?"

"Give over." Bronte rolled her eyes.

"I think it was Horace."

"And he's from Germany?"

"I think so."

They met Andy, the student of slugs and Eileen's current squeeze, just outside the restaurant. The two met with a natural flow of couples years old, hands touching arms and reaching up for a kiss. Andy was a tall, lanky bean pole, in jeans, T-shirt and a second hand jacket from a charity shop. He had shaggy hair that was mostly brushed forward over his forehead to frame a young boy's face.

"You all right?"

"Yeah."

Bronte loitered on the pavement like a spare part.

"Andy, this is my pal Bronte, I was telling you about her."

The young couple – and Christ they made her feel old, her thirty-one to their mid twenties – beamed at her.

"Nice to meet you."

"You too."

"Well, come on in you two," he said, inviting them as if they were new to the town. "Everyone else is already at the table and raring to go. We're starving."

Eileen slipped in under Andy's arm; Bronte took the door from Andy and followed the pair in. A waiter nodded to them, probably relived the last of the party had finally arrived and they might get the order taken soon. Bronte felt nervous, but reminded herself she was supposed to be a grown woman now. She'd never been that good in social situations, and her confidence waned in inverse proportion to the number of people present. It never helped when she didn't know anyone.

"Hey guys, we're finally here!" Eileen cheered to the merry band who raised glasses and beer bottles in greeting. As if she and Bronte were the intrepid explorers who had the furthest to come. "And this is my friend, Bronte, I was telling you all about. She actually lives in the heritage site."

Eileen grabbed onto Bronte's arm and pulled her forward. Bronte smiled like an awkward fool, feeling the penetration of so many eyes examining her. The bug under the microscope. Can we button hole her quickly; figure out which drawer she belongs to? Bronte's eyes drifted over the gathering. It was such an eclectic mix; had she seen all these people walking down a street she would never have guessed they all socialised together.

"So, Andy you already know," Eileen started, as if Andy and Bronte had spent more than those five seconds out on the street in each other's company. Andy leaned over the table as he manoeuvred into the end seat. The group was at a long rectangular table, and although Andy was taking what might have been head of the table, he looked rather subservient to the strange looking man at the opposite end.

Eileen started introductions up the table, skipping over the empty seat next to Andy's far side that had her name on it. "So we have Sarah here, who's really into her spiders."

Sarah looked like a cyber punk. Her long hair was cut in angles and dyed in streaks of raven black and candy pink, tied up in pigtails. She had several facial piercings, far outnumbering Bronte's little nose stud, with nasal, eyebrow, lip and multiple ear piercings, and the hint of a tattoo creeping up to her neck from under the short sleeved T shirt she wore. Sarah gave Bronte a wan smile that didn't reach her eyes. "I'm an arachnaologist. Oh my god, you're not the friend that's terrified of spiders are you?" she asked with distain she didn't try to hide.

Thank you, Eileen, Bronte thought, plastering a fake smile on her face. "It's just a phobia..."

Sarah looked as though she'd spat in her drink.

"Then we have Matthew who's in charge of the department, and his wife Emma..."

Matthew looked like the perfect boffin, with a near pudding bowl hair cut that was neatly brushed, thick plastic glasses, immaculately ironed shirt that wouldn't have looked odd with braces, and most probably cord trousers under the table. He would have been in his forties, perhaps close to fifty, as was his wife, the smiling and pleasant Emma, with blonde lightly permed hair that seemed to bounce with every breath. They both nodded politely, smiled and muttered half audible greetings.

"At the head of the table we've got Yatt."

"Yatt?" Bronte repeated the name without thinking, her tone suggesting it was a riddle. Yatt was at the opposite end of the table to Andy, and most definitely looked like the head of the group, although he couldn't have been if Matthew was in charge of the department. Matthew was the academic and Yatt looked as though he'd recently escaped from the Siberian forests of northern Russia. He had a great head of red-copper hair that was brushed back from his face, a beard and piercing round dark eyes. He was slouched back in his chair, casual in a lumberjack chequered shirt and with a hand around a beer bottle. He had a mad look, as if he would say what he wanted when he wanted, just as he did what he wanted and looked at what he wanted, and just anyone try and stop him.

"Játvarður Arvidsson," he introduced himself, his tongue flowing nimbly over the arrangement of sounds that immediately felt unpronounceable and too long to remember for English speakers. He looked incredibly serious, almost as if he was daring Bronte to try and repeat his name, get it wrong, insult his forefathers and suffer the consequences. Suddenly and disconcertingly he broke out into a grin. "I'm Icelandic." As if that explained everything. "You Brits struggle with my name so people call me Yatt. Isn't that so, Eileen?"

"Yeah, yeah, yeah. Yatt's into spiders as well."

That solicited a loud laugh from the end of the table.

The man sitting next to the empty seat destined for Bronte spoke. "I don't know what the problem is. I can say your name. Játvarður Arvidsson." He had that perfect English with a hint of American and lazy unconcern of linguistic greatness that could only be Dutch.

"Yes, but you're not English," Yatt called back to him.

"This is Horace," Eileen started.

"Horst," the man corrected, twisting in his seat to assess Bronte. "Horst Van Det Bruuk. I'm over from Amsterdam."

Eileen blushed lightly, realising she'd utterly misremembered his details. "And you're into..?"

"Into?" Horst raised his eyebrows at her. "What do you mean? Like hobbies. I like drinking beer, windsurfing and collecting butterflies..."

"Stop it!" the woman sitting next to him playfully slapped his arm.

"Is this meant to be the dating game?" Sarah muttered into her cider.

Bronte wished a sinkhole could appear right under her feet.

"I study myrmecology," he said, watching Bronte's face closely to see if she would have the faintest idea what he was talking about. "Specifically ant social structures."

"And next to Horst we've got Anna Maria, who's the butterfly lady."

Anna Maria, a rosy cheeked blonde with the healthy glow of someone who spent a lot of time trawling through meadows with her long bronzed legs, smiled genuinely at Bronte.

"And then finally there's Janet and Robbie," Eileen pointed out the couple sitting to Yatt's left. "Janet's into dung beetles, and Robbie's..."

"I'm a hanger-on who knows fuck all about bugs," the man took over, leaning over the back of Anna Maria and Horst to shake hands with Bronte. "You, me, Eileen and Emma are the only sane people here, believe me."

"I'd say you were lying but you're not the first today to call me insane," Yatt said.

The waiter hovered up behind Bronte possibly closer than was appropriate.

"Can I hand out menus now the party is gathered?"

Bronte dropped eagerly down into her chair between Andy and Horst, keen to get out of the limelight. Hopefully they'd all go back to discussing bugs and she could regain her balance. She needed to consider the all important decision of the day: what she was going to eat.

The waiter dealt out the menus with a speed that suggested he'd do well on poker tables. Bronte opened the menu, trying to look engrossed in it, all the time with that prickling sensation she was being observed.

"Bronte."

Her name was spoken like a command. She looked up to see the wild man of the north staring unapologetically at her. He sat forward in his chair with his elbows on the table.   "I've not heard this name before here. Is this Bronte like the writing sisters?"

"Oh yeah," Eileen piped up. "I'd never thought of that, just that your name's a bit weird."

"You don't have sisters called Charlotte and Emily do you?" Anna Maria added, genuinely meaning to be friendly but only adding to Bronte's general discomfort.

"No, I don't have any sisters. My mother's Emily."

"Your mother is Emily Bronte?" Horst looked bewildered.

"Well, no, Bronte's my first name. My mother's Emily Campbell."

"So just a coincidence?"

"No, my mother went through a Bronte sisters obsession when she was having us..."

"Us being?"

"Me and my brother, Branwell."

"Your brother's called Branwell?" Anna Maria sounded delighted with this. "That's so cute, Bronte and Branwell. No, wait a minute. You don't mean Branwell Campbell, do you?"

"I think she does," Yatt looked over at Anna Maria as if she was mad. "She's given you all the clues."

"No, but I've worked with your brother before now. Down in Wiltshire a couple of summers ago. He manages a chalk land wildlife reserve there. If it is the same Branwell Campbell. I can't imagine there's many people with that name."

"That's my brother."

"Wow, this is such a small world!" Anna Maria beamed. "And how's he doing? Is he still down there?"

Bronte shook her head. "Branwell's always getting itchy feet. He's got a new job recently; he's away up to Skye now."

"That so doesn't surprise me. He was such an engaged, enthusiastic guy. You know these people you meet, and you just know they're going to do great things..."

"Sounds like you've got a bit of a crush, Anna Maria," Yatt teased.

"Oh no, just the greatest professional respect," she said, a blush rolling up her neck from her chest. "It's good to know there are still passionate conservationists out there."

Horst looked as though his interest had been sparked, and he looked at Bronte with fresh eyes. "And do you also work in the environment, conservation, land management and such, Bronte?"

"No. As Eileen kindly mentioned, I have a phobia."

"So perhaps you are a botanist?"

"No, I didn't do anything like that." She was starting to feel disconcerted, almost drunk, as she was putting in her order with the waiter whilst trying to answer the questions. She was aware those eyes and minds were making assumptions, and the wrong ones now that they knew she was Branwell's sister. Assuming she was destined for greatness. "I work at the mill."

"The mill?" Horst's eyebrows knitted. "Do you mean like a windmill? You're in flour production."

"No, the mill, Salt Mill here in Saltaire. The big building by the train station. Did you come here by train?"

"Yes, we came on the train from Leeds. I saw this long building. So it's a mill, but not to grind flour?"

"It used to be a fabric mill, but they stopped production in the eighties. It's been converted into space for businesses and galleries now."

"Eileen works in the cafe there," Andy threw in to the mix.

"You work in a cafe?" The expectant light behind Horst's eyes was starting to dim.

"No, I work in the bookshop. It's on the same floor as Eileen's cafe..." she added lamely.

"So you work in retail," Sarah surmised in a flat tone.

"Yes, I..."

"So your parents didn't encourage you to get an education like your brother?" Horst was back with the questions.

Bronte let out a long breath. She really disliked people who made assumptions about people based on the job they happened to be doing at that moment. Or the way they would look at people in retail, people in routine office jobs or serving in a restaurant, as though they were a bit dumb, a bit lacking in imagination, and had just kind of slumped in life. She could see from Horst's changing expressions that the longer this conversation-cross-inquisition went on the more disappointed he was with this meal neighbour. Perhaps not the tasty morsel he'd been promised. "Yes, I got an education, and yes, I work in a book shop at the moment."

"So you got a degree?" Horst sounded as though there might be some hope for her. "Did you go into natural sciences like your brother, or some other branch of academia?"

"I did fine art."

"Fine art?" He didn't sound impressed. "That's like..."

"Painting pictures," Sarah finished for them.

"I think it's really good," Anna Maria said, leaning forward so she could see Bronte. "I wish I had the talent to draw."

"It's not really proper degree material, though is it?" Sarah continued. "Not like you have to study, write essays, produce original thought."

"Sarah," Yatt growled before muttering something in Icelandic. "You should be thankful for the artists. Otherwise you'd have nothing other than 'egg-fried rice' in Chinese to tattoo on your backside."

"Well, at least I know how to behave at academic occasions," Sarah retorted.

Matthew, or rather Professor Matthew Hickman, head of department, to give him his full title, placed his hands down on the table, giving an attempt at authority that was not particularly convincing. Even before he spoke he knew no one would listen. "Now, children..."

"Woah!" Bronte gasped as the waiter leaned over to put her fruit cider in front of her, sloshing a good third into her lap.

"Oh, madam, I'm so sorry," The waiter said, instinctively pulling back her chair as she went to get up. "I'll get you another drink, on the house of course."

On her feet, her dress dripping between her flip flops, Bronte felt as though she'd wet herself. "I'm just going to wash this off," she muttered, leaving the table and heading for the ladies toilets.

As she passed the bar at the back of the restaurant, the waiter who had thrown her drink over her stepped up. "Sorry about that love, it was a bit impulsive. Sounded like you were getting an earful from those pompous twats. Thought I'd diffuse the situation for you."

"By pouring my drink on me?"

"It was impulsive."

"It gave me an excuse to go to the ladies."

"There'll be a fresh unspilled drink waiting for you when you get back."

In the ladies toilets she stood at the sink, splashing water at her dress. It was silk. When it dried there'd be a tide mark until she washed the entire thing. She was going to look ridiculous. She met her eye in the mirror. I'd rather be at home now, she thought. I want to be at home hanging out with my imaginary spider that I'm supposed to be terrified of. How pathetic.

Eileen stumbled into the ladies as Bronte was pressing herself in odd ways against the wall to try and dry the front of her dress under the hand drier.

"Bronte, are you all right? I don't know what that was all about. Honestly, they're a really nice bunch. I didn't get any attitude because I 'just' work in a cafe. Seriously." She leant her back against the wall. "No one's wanted to check up on my academic credentials."

Bronte waved it off. "It's fine. People are curious."

"I think Horst's a bit of an intellectual snob. Sorry."

"No worries."

"Although that atmosphere, man. Sarah's such a rude bitch."

"I don't suppose art seems all that academic when you're measuring spider legs or whatever groundbreaking work it is they do." The two women shared a look and started giggling.

"Don't worry; she's an arsey bitch to everyone, from what Andy tells me. Did you hear how she spoke to Yatt? I mean, she's just a student doing her Masters like Andy. Yatt's staff. You'd think there'd be a bit of respect there. Well, I shouldn't tell you this because it's unverified gossip, but apparently Sarah got a bit drunk at Christmas and tried it on with Yatt."

"The mad woodsman?"

"He's bonkers, but he's all right. He's Andy's tutor. Anyway, Yatt told Sarah to fuck off, and she's been this angry scorned woman ever since."

"What a lovely bunch of people you've brought me to meet."

"They are good fun. Come on, we'll just ignore Sarah. And hopefully Horst'll get the stick out of his arse. He's all right looking, isn't he? And he windsurfs. Nice body." Eileen waggled her eyebrows.

Bronte ignored the innuendo. "I'll be out in a minute. I just want to get these dry enough so I don't have a wet dress plastered to my thighs all evening."

She watched Eileen trot back out of the ladies, and during the evening whenever she looked over in Eileen and Andy's direction, she realised just how involved Eileen already was. Eileen was usually a casual relationship girl, but she was falling fast with this one. The two of them snuggled up together at the end of the table, Eileen talking about Andy's fellow students and tutors the way a wife did about a husband's work colleagues. She hoped it would last, because this was going to be a broken heart if it all went wrong.

The evening settled down, and as the alcohol flowed the atmosphere dispersed and friends and colleagues got involved in ongoing conversations. The table wasn't the best for casual conversations between all guests, and as Horst lost interest in Bronte, and Eileen and Andy snuggled closer together, Bronte was left with a choice of either trying to chat with Sarah, who was pointedly ignoring her, or slowly chewing over her food whilst she contemplated life. She took the latter.

By ten o'clock everyone was finished and the bill had been passed to the most responsible person, Matthew. The group was talking about going on to a couple of local pubs Eileen had recommended. Bronte found the right cash in her bag and pushed her share of the bill across the table to Matthew.

"I'm going to have to head off now. I'm working a full shift tomorrow," she said her apologies, Matthew and Emma smiling and saying they were sorry she had to head off early in that inoffensive, politely retiring way that such people mastered.

Bronte abruptly got up out of her chair. She wasn't good at crowds and this evening felt like a failure. "It was nice meeting you all," she said, although most probably didn't hear. She turned and hurried out of the restaurant before anyone had any chance to make comments about shop work, or her happy-defensive mask slipped.

Out onto the main road the cooler air hit her, a sudden slap of freshness. She started to hurry as well as one could in flip flops, eager to get down a side street and out of sight before they started to pour out of the restaurant in search of the first pub. As she hurried she felt her hair loosening further, the paintbrush and hair pin slipping out. She pulled them out of her tangle of hair, shaking her head to loosen her hair. How ridiculous she must have looked, turning up with a paintbrush in her hair. It wasn't as if anyone else had arrived with such appendages: a butterfly in the hair, a spider in the beard, bees in their bonnets... Bronte ran a hand over her face and put the paintbrush and pin in her bag. She was thirty one years old and she still had moments of a silly girl-child lacking in confidence. There were people her age with several kids. Mortgages. Careers. Businesses. Into properly adult phases of life, and she was still bumbling around in the dark.

Bronte wasn't a dim wit, but faced with serious academia, and the intelligent conversation master Horst, her brain had short circuited and she couldn't think of much to say at all. He'd tried with her, but given up and focused on Anna Maria who could talk for hours about the butterfly aerodynamics project she was working on with the aircraft engineering industry.

When did I give up on myself, Bronte wondered, or was there never very much to champion? Oh Christ, she needed to stop feeling so bloody sorry for herself. She was an intelligent, independent and artistic woman, who had nothing to be ashamed of. There were people who wanted to spend time with her. Just when had she started disappearing into her retreat?

"Bronte!"

She snapped out of her self-pity and saw Paul Warren ambling up the street towards her.

"I am very glad to see you," he said, his expression full of genuine appreciation. "I was just thinking how I'm heading up to the pub to see the same old tired faces, and then I saw you heading my way, and I thought thank God!"

"Paul, you old flatterer."

"Seriously Bronte, don't do yourself down. Any sane man would be glad of some time in your company. You heading my way?"

"I was just going home."

"I thought you said you'd come out to the pub with me this weekend."

"I never said..."

He broke out into an easy smile. "I know, I know, I'm putting words into your mouth." He studied her face as if he wanted to get better acquainted with her mouth. "So are you coming?"

"I've got a shift tomorrow."

"Me too."

She couldn't remember which pubs the insect group were going to, and she certainly didn't want to bump into them again.

She wasn't in the mood for noise and crowds of people. She wanted to be home.

"You look sad, Bronte. Shitty evening?"

"Ah, it's nothing."

"Whoever they are, they ain't worth it. Come on," he said, slinging an arm around her shoulders. "I'll walk you home."

"Got to dash, babe."

A quick kiss on her cheek.

"This shirt stinks of smoke, I need to go home and change before work."

"Not even a cup of tea?"

"Afraid not."

Another kiss on her cheek, then Paul Warren was heading out of the back door, through the little yard and into the alley as if sneaking away from a secret rendez vous. It was Sunday and it was still early. No one would be up at this time.

Bronte stood at the kitchen window and watched him go, hugging her dressing gown to her body. She had succumbed. She had let Paul Warren seduce her. She had listened to the honey he poured into her ear, the attention he gave her and the affection when he'd made his way into the living room yesterday evening. She'd been feeling sorry for herself, lonely and a little vulnerable. The timing had hit bull's-eye and she had been unable to resist. He'd made her feel special, desirable, and beautiful. At least it had felt that way through the drunken haze of talk, smiles and flashes of lustful looks. Up in the bedroom under the sweaty humping it hadn't seemed quite so amazing, and Bronte with her often distracted mind, had found herself staring at the shadows on the ceiling whilst she'd waited for him to come. Was this what she had been waiting for?

Still, no relationship was just about the sex, she reminded herself. The banter had been really good last night, and he'd been so affectionate and good humoured. Good fun. Slightly more disinterested this morning though.

Bronte turned away from the window. George was standing on the worktop beside the kettle.

"That was Paul Warren," she told the spider, still enjoying that warm buzz inside as if she had a boyfriend. "He was nice, wasn't he?"

George turned and vomited a partially digested fly onto the worktop.

Bronte's smile drooped. "Or not."

George scurried around the curve of worktops to the sink in that unnatural movement of eight legs, like a demonic dismembered hand, and went up to the window, tapping a couple of legs against the glass. Even though she had grown used to George, and increasingly found herself searching him out when she was at home, she still felt that touch of icy horror across her back whenever she watched him running about.

"You want to be out?" She unlatched the window and let the spider out.

"You all go off and leave me," she sighed, mooching over to the kettle to make a cup of tea. She wondered for a moment when Paul would call, and then she remembered that she was still living in reality. Paul would never call. Paul didn't do relationships, only conquests. And although there potentially could be occasional nights now and then when their paths crossed and he was feeling randy and she was feeling low, the edge had been shaved off. He had taken her, another cross in the box. She was just another shag. And although she had taken Eileen's advice and gone for it, taken the next invitation and tried to shake things up in her life a bit, she wasn't convinced she felt any the better for it.

"Just another easy lay," she grumbled, taking her tea into the living room.

How pathetic.

Life returned to its routines. As Bronte had predicted, Paul Warren neither called nor made any attempt to make a date with her. If she had been stupid enough to think she might have been the 'special one' before he slept with her, she was too old now to hang on to any hope that a great romance had been about to blossom. He'd got a check box ticked on his list and her life continued as though precious little had happened.

Days and customers merged through the work at the bookshop, and time lost meaning to the point where an hour or a month could have just passed. It was impossible to tell. At home she still saw her imaginary friend, George, and assumed whatever issue her subconscious was trying to work out remained unresolved. She threw herself back into her art, taking up black and white illustrations with india ink. She had thought of doing a series of domestic scenes for blank greetings cards she could persuade Lillian to sell in the shop. And whilst originally she had thought of basing the rooms on tidier versions of her own home, the cute scenes swiftly took a queerer turn when she was unable to keep herself from adding George somewhere amongst the depicted clutter. One evening she left the materials on the kitchen table to go to the bathroom. When she returned she found George tentatively dipping a couple of feet into the ink well before skittering across a blank sheet of paper and looking back in consternation before almost wiping his feet on the edge of the sheet. She vaguely remembered reading somewhere that spiders tasted through their feet and wondered what ink was like.

Another Sunday found her perfectly awake at five in the morning and unable to settle. She tossed and turned in bed before giving up and heading downstairs. She needed to get out of the house. Opening a shoulder bag on the table, she moved around the house gathering art materials before making a flask of coffee to take with her. She didn't notice George slinking into the shadowy confines of the bag, and snapped the handles together in her hand before slinging the bag over her shoulder and leaving the house.

She dropped down onto the little cobbled road running adjacent to the railway tracks and went up to the hill road, following it down to the river and canal. Crossing over the bridges, she walked into the formal Victorian park, fresh with dew and early morning bird calls. It was empty of people aside from a solitary jogger she could see pounding the ground at the wide stretch of grass by the river. Bronte went up to the higher level of the park, and sat down near the bandstand.

Setting her bag on the ground at her feet, she let out a small scream when she opened it and saw George's large blue eyes staring back up at her. She scrambled back along the bench on instinct. Even though she knew George wasn't real, and she was accustomed to him from their co-habitation, her subconscious couldn't switch off that spider-terror. The hairy pom pom on eight legs crawled out of the bag and stepped onto the tarmac footpath, testing the air before scuttling off to a shrubbery.

"It's a good thing you're not real," Bronte muttered after his retreating figure. "Or else I probably shouldn't be letting you lose out here."

She settled back against the bench and lifted up the bag, now that she was confident it was spider free. She enjoyed the early morning emptiness whilst slowly drinking her coffee, and took out her sketchpad to start some idle drawings. She glanced back up the path to see George amble out of the undergrowth and stop on the side of the path. The feeling of heavy thudding vibrated up all eight legs. The oversized tarantula turned its back to Bronte and stared up at the creature bounding towards him. The jogger, whose ears were full of thumping dance music matching the pace he wanted to run at, and eyes focused on the stats from his electronic health monitoring wrist band, went straight past George without giving him a second glance.

Of course the jogger wouldn't give George a second glance. George wasn't actually there. She still gave him a shout and let him crawl back into her bag when she was ready to leave.

By the afternoon Bronte was stretched out on the sofa idly reading a book. There was music playing, the sort of lazy summer chill out music that simply called for a half-drunken smile of satisfaction to be plastered over everyone's faces. George was on the coffee table messing about with some wool remnants from old knitting projects.

The front doorbell rang. Grumbling at the disturbance, Bronte looked around for a suitable bookmark, failed, and ended up hanging the book on the back of the sofa, open at the page she was at. She pulled herself onto her bare feet and padded through the living room to the door.

"Bronte!" Eileen was on the doorstep, giddy and smiling. She looked particularly dolled up, with bright red lipstick and a patterned vintage red dress on.

"Eileen."

"I'm just bringing those CDs back." She pulled out a couple of CDs from her bag. "I'm meeting Andy at the station in ten minutes."

"Oh right, do you want to come in and wait?" The station was only a minute's walk from Bronte's home.

"Sure. You all right?"

"Yeah, just having a lazy Sunday. A bit of drawing, a bit of reading." Bronte wandered into the living room, flicking through the CD albums Eileen had returned. She'd lent them that long ago she'd almost forgotten she'd ever owned them. "You and Andy up to anything this afternoon? You're looking very nice today."

The expected babbling wasn't forthcoming. Bronte turned around to see Eileen still in the doorway. The girl looked as though she was about to throw up. "What the hell is going on?"

"Nothing, it's Sunday."

"Bronte!" Eileen whined in a high pitched voice. She looked as though she was about to burst into tears. "What the fuck is that on your table?"

"That's just George." A connection was made in her consciousness and Bronte took a long step backwards to the kitchen doorway. She looked over at Eileen. "My imaginary friend."

"Who the hell has a spider as an imaginary friend?"

"You can see him?" Bronte's eyes filled up with tears and she felt her limbs start to shake. "You can see..."

Eileen nodded.

She'd believed he was imaginary. The jogger had run straight past him. Albert had never seen him, for every time he'd been by, George had somehow vanished. She'd decided he was part of her imagination. She'd opened the kitchen window, her arm so close George could have reached out with his legs and tapped her. She'd walked through town with him in a shoulder bag, like one of those blonde bimbos with a Chihuahua in her designer handbag.

George, who'd had his back to the women all this time, sensed a charge in the air and turned around, first looking at Bronte, then at the stranger in the front door.

"What the hell?" Eileen gasped as the round blue eyes stared up at her. "What the hell is it?"

"It's a spider."

"How the hell are you living in the same house as this?"

"I thought it was imaginary. I thought I was going mad."

"How could you think this was imaginary?"

"I don't know." Bronte wiped at her eyes with the back of her hand. Tears were an automatic terror reaction.

Eileen looked from Bronte to the spider who continued sorting the wool. "It's the size of a fucking cat."

"I know," Bronte whispered.

"How long have you been living with this?"

"A few weeks."

She gazed about the room, the casual domesticity, the open book on the back of the soda. Bronte, a self confessed hysterical archnophobe, had been lying on the sofa chilling out whilst a giant monster spider pottered about on the coffee table. All because she had somehow convinced herself that it wasn't real.

Eileen looked from the spider to Bronte. "You called it George."

"That's his name."

Eileen breathed deeply through her nose, gathering her thoughts. "You've been living with this beast for weeks. It can't be dangerous then, can it?"

"Maybe it can smell fear. Do you think spiders can smell?"

"I don't know. Look, Andy's train is arriving. I'll go get Andy. He'll know what to do."

Andy's first reaction on stepping through the door and catching sight of George was to yell, "Woah, fuck me!" and stagger back into Eileen who had been following him into the building.

"Andy!" Eileen whacked him on the arse. "Don't be such a baby."

"Have you seen the size of that thing?"

"You study bugs."

"I do slugs."

Bronte was slouched in the kitchen doorway. Although the initial stress of realising George was a real spider had worn off, she still hadn't quite found her old confidence to flop back down on the sofa with her book. George was still on the coffee table, and after Eileen had gone and the screeching had ceased, had returned to sorting wool remnants, or whatever it was he thought he was doing. With the noisy arrival of Eileen and Andy, he stopped and froze in position, tentatively watching the main entrance.

"Look at those eyes. It's unreal. It looks like a bloody stuffed toy."

"What kind of toy looks like that? Have you seen its legs?" Eileen muttered.

"Are you sure it's real?"

"I didn't knit it," Bronte said.

Andy got his phone out of his back trouser pocket and flicked through on the screen to get to the video function. "I'm going to have to film it." He started filming, slowly moving into the room and around the side of the sofa. "You two aren't having me on; it's not just a model?"

George took a step back as the stranger approached.

"It moves. Jesus. I've never seen anything like it. Those eyes are way too big for a spider. It's got to be a robot."

"Does Bronte look like the kind of girl who could make a robot like that?" Eileen, remaining at the front door, asked. Bronte gave her a sharp look that was missed. What was that supposed to mean?

"This is insane," Andy tittered nervously, going in for a close up. He was on edge, expecting the spider to jump or attack. He was able to get closer and closer until the spider's face filled up the screen on his phone. At this vicinity George got curious and lifted up a couple of legs in that macabre pianist movement spiders are so good at. Andy involuntarily jumped and dropped the phone in the strands of wool. George reversed to the far end of the coffee table.

Andy laughed to cover his jitters. "It's not dangerous, is it?"

"I have no idea."

Eileen folded her arms. "I can't believe you thought you were imagining that thing."

"What was I supposed to think?" Bronte said defensively. "Andy's right, George looks like a toy. And every time I got Albert over, he just disappeared."

"Who's Albert?"

"My next door neighbour. He comes over sometimes to get rid of spiders for me." Bronte grimaced as George plopped down from the coffee table and started to run for the kitchen doorway. She pressed her back up against the door frame and stood on one foot, feeling too scared to run away.

Andy had his phone again and was filming George's fluid movement. He stumbled around the sofa, too busy staring at the screen to keep an eye on real life, and caught Bronte's panic on screen before following George's hairy rump into the kitchen. Brushing past Bronte, Andy filmed George climb up the kitchen cupboard, and to the mug tree. There was a chink of ceramics as George climbed up into the oversized novelty tea mug, reversing inside and leaving legs to dangle outside. Big blue eyes watched cautiously. Andy finished on that view, before stopping the film.

"I have to email this right now," he said to no one in particular, an excited schoolboy as he jabbed away at the phone's screen. "We've got to get someone in to look at this. I mean, man..." his giddy thoughts were failed by his tongue as he retreated into his phone.

Bronte felt a foreboding of a different kind. George was real. Andy was sending off videos alerting other people in the world that George existed. What exactly were they starting?

"What are you working tomorrow, Bronte?"

"Hours, you mean? I finish at half five."

"Do you mind if I come back tomorrow with one of the arachnid guys? They are going to go ape over this."

"I suppose." Bronte didn't sound enthusiastic.

"Brilliant."

Eileen was checking the time on her phone. "Andy, we should be heading off."

"Yeah, yeah, sure." He couldn't take his eyes off George. "I'll see you tomorrow, Bronte, half five."

Eileen and Andy left. Only Bronte and George remained in the house. She supposed it was all safe, given that Andy, a bug expert, hadn't asked her if she'd be all right in the house alone with a giant spider. She'd managed the last couple of weeks in deluded oblivion. Another day ought not to be a problem. And then what? Would they want to take George away? She felt a strange lump in her throat at that thought, and a surge of possessiveness. It wasn't up to them, just because they were academics didn't mean they could tell her what to do. Then she remembered Sarah, the sniffy arachnaologist who had sneered down at Bronte the entire dinner. She really didn't want Sarah in her home, the pathetic home of someone who worked in retail, whilst bagging up her spider and leaving in judgement.

Bronte felt her lower lip curl in disgust. She looked at the mug tree. George stared back, his blue eyes seemingly shiner than usual as if he was about to burst into tears. You're going to let them take me away, aren't you?

"Stop being ridiculous," she snapped. It wasn't clear who she was talking to.

There was no one waiting at her house after work the following day. Perhaps they had decided Andy's film was a joke, or they just had better things to do. Or Sarah had curled up her toes and declared nothing on earth, not even the scientific discovery of the century, would persuade her to visit Bronte Campbell.

Bronte hurried into the house and through to the kitchen. George was standing motionless on the window sill, but started to tap against the glass as soon as the vibrations of Bronte's footsteps moved through the house. She rushed over to the window and opened it. At least if he was out, no one would be able to take him away.

She went back through to the living room, put a CD on for company and sank onto the sofa. It would be the end of the summer holidays. No one would want to come out to Saltaire. Andy had probably forgotten about it. He and Eileen would have gotten drunk last night, and that would be the end of things.

The doorbell rang.

Bronte closed her eyes. What had she done to deserve this? Andy was Eileen's boyfriend. As girlfriend, it was Eileen's cross to bear to suffer the annoying friends and unimpressed in-laws. Bronte shouldn't be dragged into that at all.

Begrudgingly she pulled herself back onto her feet and went to answer the front door.

"Bronte!" Andy sounded over enthusiastic and slightly panicky. He was scrubbed and hair brushed, with a fresh T shirt showing a cartoon slug giving the finger to anyone who cared to look.

Bronte looked for Sarah and was so relived to note her absence that she felt her tense shoulders drop a couple of centimetres. Just behind Andy waited Yatt, the wild man of Iceland and Andy's dissertation tutor. He looked a little bored, as if there were better things he could be doing than being dragged around Saltaire on a wild goose chase. Although Andy was specialising in slugs, she remembered now that Eileen had mentioned Yatt's specialisation was spiders. Her heart sank though, as it looked as though his mood wasn't much better than what she had been expecting from Sarah.

"Good Afternoon, Bronte," he greeted her tiredly. "I'm Yatt; I met you a couple of weeks ago."

"I remember."

"And you didn't strike me as the kind of person who would take part in such nonsense."

She opened her mouth, but found herself dumb from his disappointment. He was virtually a stranger and yet the directness found its target and scratched at her.

"Andy emailed me this video he has concocted. I was surprised you had agreed to act in it. But then first impressions can be misleading."

It was as if he was accusing her of treachery. "I haven't done anything."

"Yatt thinks the video is a fake," Andy explained.

"You can create anything on computers these days."

A man walking his dog along the street gave Bronte a curious look. "Maybe you two should come in," she suggested. "But it's not a fake. I thought I was imagining it, but Eileen and Andy saw him."

The two men entered her home and Bronte closed the front door. The trio loitered awkwardly in the living room. Yatt looked irritated, Andy sheepish, and Bronte felt as though she was the chief instigator to all this trouble.

"There are no spiders that look like that thing," Yatt started up again. "And I have better things to do with my holidays that take part in stupid practical jokes..."

"No one forced you to come here." The words were out of her mouth before she had taken a moment to consider them. She wasn't usually this abrupt with people. Yatt stopped talking and both men looked at her, a little surprised by her reaction.

Yatt's scowl relented. "Very well, I'm sorry. I apologise that Andy has involved you in this nonsense. And you're right, you haven't nagged me to drive out to Saltaire." He gave his student a stern look.

"It's not nonsense," Andy retorted, peering about the living room. "So where is he?"

"George?"

Yatt raised his eyebrows. "This is the spider?"

"His name is George. He's out at the moment."

Yatt clapped his hands together once. "Well, this is convenient. I'll just have to take Andy's poorly filmed clip as evidence."

Andy was increasingly uncomfortable, feeling like a foolish boy rather than being taken seriously as the scientist he considered himself to be. Even the T shirt wasn't helping his credibility. "What do you mean he's out?"

"He goes out every day."

"Where?"

"I don't know."

"Well, can you not shout him back in or something?"

"Ha, you're telling me he's a dog now?" Yatt laughed.

Bronte looked bemused. "I've never had to. He just strolls back in when he's ready. I suppose I could try."

Yatt was shaking his head in despairing amusement. "Very well, let's go and shout your spider back in."

Was this how people had felt in the past when they were told to walk the gangplank, Bronte wondered. She led the way through to the kitchen, pausing to unlock the back door. She could feel Andy's desperation without even having to look at him. She really wanted George back in the house, if only so that Yatt would stop looking at her as if she were an idiot. She stepped out of the house and into the yard. Yatt stood in the doorway, looking about her little yard as if to say, well, crazy woman, where are all of your monster spiders? Bronte's heart sank further when she saw the puffs of smoke twist up from next door and she realised Albert was sat outside smoking his pipe. Could this get any worse? Another witness to her humiliation. All the students and doctors and professors of bugs would sit around in the lab and laugh about this day. Fine art students, what did they know about anything?

"Now then, Bronte," Albert greeted her. "Pleasant afternoon."

Bronte closed her eyes. He had seen her.

"Call him in," Yatt commanded.

Albert twisted in consternation at the sound of a man's voice coming from Bronte's house. His eyebrows rose when he saw Yatt, with his flaming red hair, bristling beard and piercing eyes. Not what he had expected, but then Bronte did have funny taste in everything. "Afternoon," he nodded to Yatt. "Who are you calling in?" to Bronte.

"George," she said quietly, not able to look at Yatt or Albert.

"He will only have small ears; you'll have to shout louder than that." Yatt sounded as though he was enjoying this.

I am a fool, Bronte thought. Just an utter fool. Then she felt angry over the automatic assumption was that she was a fool. It was more obvious to believe Bronte was an idiot than that the story of George might be true. Screw them all. She glared at Albert's birch tree. "George!" she yelled, the war cry painfully out of place in this little back alley of Saltaire.

"George?" Albert repeated. "You been getting a dog now?"

There was rustling in the birch tree, then something brown threw itself down from the boughs and into Bronte's yard. It ran across the ground, scrambled up the wall and through the open kitchen window. A final nimble leap brought it to the middle of the kitchen table.

Thank god, Bronte thought.

There was a clatter as Albert dropped his pipe. Yatt broke out into something in Icelandic that had the tone of swearing.

"See?" Andy was the first to speak. Even though he had met George before, and was a student of the insect and arachnid world, he kept a safe distance from the table, retreating to the living room door.

"What is it?" Yatt breathed as he went back into the kitchen.

"I thought you were the spider doctor."

"Where did you get it?"

"He just appeared in my house."

"This can't be someone's pet; there isn't a spider like it." Yatt picked up one of Bronte's paintbrushes from the side and sat down at the end of the kitchen table. The doctor of arachnids and the spider regarded one another in quiet awe.

"You think it's one of those Brazilian bird eating tarantulas?" Andy asked.

"It looks like a tarantula, yet the body is more bulbous, and the volume of hair is nothing I've ever seen on a spider. But the legs almost make me think more of a huntsman."

"God almighty." Albert, who had heaved himself over the wall between his and Bronte's yard, peered over Bronte's shoulder into the kitchen. "I thought you were having me on when you said there was a giant spider in the house."

"We all thought she was joking." Yatt reached out to the spider with the studious calm of a surgeon, and gently slipped the paintbrush behind George's front two legs. He lifted the brush up so he could tilt George's body upwards, to get a better look at the mouth and underside. This wasn't a robot or anything artificially created. "I lived in Brazil for six years and I never saw anything like this."

George was growing tired of being propped up at an odd angle. He was not distressed, for there was a calm atmosphere in the room and the creature before him was giving no signs of panic. He started to move, stepping over the paintbrush and towards Yatt.

Bronte and Albert winced in horror from the back door as the spider strolled up to Yatt, placing a couple of feet upon his forearm that rested on the table. Two hairy legs upon one hairy forearm, the light glinting off Yatt's coppery arm hairs. George blinked as if he couldn't quite believe what he was seeing. Yatt burst out into Icelandic again and George reversed swiftly away from him.

Bronte felt herself let go of her breath now the spider wasn't perched on Yatt's arm. She didn't know how he could have done that without screaming.

Yatt looked up at her in wonder. "George blinked."

Why was that amazing? Bronte shrugged. "He does that. He even shuts his eyes when he goes to sleep," she added flippantly.

"Spiders don't have eyelids. They can't shut their eyes. This is just..."

Whatever it was, George had enough. He jumped across to the worktop and made a bee line for the mug tree. There was a familiar tinkling sound as he backed into his favourite mug.

"He usually sleeps in there."

Yatt was straight out of the chair and at the mug tree, peering in at George. "So this is his safe place. And this isn't a pet of yours; he just turned up in your house?"

"Yes, it was a few weeks ago."

"Do you know if anyone around here keeps exotic pets? Or have you recently had any shipments from abroad? Any parcels? Maybe even a sack of food or packet?"

Bronte was slowly shaking her head, flicking back through what little had happened in the last weeks. There had been no parcels, and she had no idea if anyone around here kept strange pets. Even if they had done, surely George would have been a species Yatt would have recognised. "Bananas," she said. "I bought bananas back when we had that hot snap. They just seemed to explode whilst I was out at work. I came back and the skins were all split and there was slime all over the worktop."

"I'm going to have to make a study of this. I'll have to speak to you more," he added as a note to Bronte, as he straightened up from peering in at the mug tree. "I'm going to have to go home, there's a lot of things I need. Are you at home tomorrow?"

"I'm working again."

"What time do you go to work?"

"Half nine."

"If I came at half eight? I don't want to impose myself in your life, but this is a massive discovery, you understand. There is so much I need to document. Would you be comfortable in leaving me alone with George all day? This is going to take days."

So many questions. Yatt had a giddy glint in his eye. This was his thing, so she supposed it was only natural he would be excited about George. But he looked like a man who had just been offered the moon. And did she want him turning up early in the morning? Was she happy leaving him alone in her house all day? Not that she had anything of particular worth stealing. Not that a university doctor would need to steal from a woman who worked in a bookshop. "Sure."

"Perfect. I'm going straight back to Leeds now to get everything together. Andy, are you wanting a lift back?"

"I suppose?" Andy looked confused by Yatt's plan.

"Thank you, Bronte," Yatt said, heading for the front door, barely able to stop a full retreat into his thoughts, planning everything he wanted to do.

Andy trotted after Yatt and caught up with him as he was unlocking the car door. "Is this a good idea?"

"Of course it is. I can't miss this study opportunity."

"No, but..." Andy had to pause to get into the passenger seat. Yatt wasn't stopping to think. "I mean leaving her alone in the house with the spider."

"You did yesterday. Besides, they've been living together for weeks."

"Shouldn't we be taking George back with us? Is it really safe to have him running around loose? If she's letting him out, you don't know what he's killing or what he's doing."

Yatt paused in starting the engine and tapped his fingers on the steering wheel. "That's a conversation I will have to have with Bronte in a few days' time. But it's precisely the reason that she's been letting him out that we'll have to continue as is for now. I need to find out exactly where George has been going. I need to know what he's been doing, taking and leaving and where before we take him away."

Andy sank back into his seat. "Yeah, I guess I didn't think about that. You know Bronte's an archnophobe, don't you? Eileen says she's terrified shitless of spiders. Has to get that old man in to deal with them."

"Which makes it all the more interesting as to why she and George are managing to live together."

"It's because he's fluffy and has big eyes." Andy decided. "Women, they can't resist anything cute."

Yatt started to laugh as he pulled out from behind a parked car. "In that case it will be double trouble when I go back tomorrow."

Andy snorted. "Yeah right."

It was drizzling when Bronte woke up. She couldn't keep to her usual morning rigmarole, weighted down with unsettled sensations. She made certain she was showered and dressed long before eight o'clock. She made a vague attempt at tidying in the living room. As she gathered up scatterings of sketchbooks, paperbacks and magazines, stacking them in neat piles, she asked herself what the hell she thought she was doing, and purposefully kicked a couple of magazines on to the floor. As long as she wasn't running downstairs to answer the door in her pyjamas, no other effort was required.

She went into the kitchen to do some art before work. Perched in the corner on a stool, she found herself distracted from her usual garden observations. Instead she had her pot of india ink on the window sill, and was drawing the view of her kitchen, focusing on the mug tree. George was still in residence, legs dangling out in all directions. Either his eyes were closed or he had gone in head first last night and it was his arse she was drawing. There was a rustle in the mug tree and two orbs popped open. No, it had been arse-first into the mug as always. She left two circles of white for eyes in her illustration.

The doorbell rang. Bronte looked at George. "Looks like your number one fan is here."

She wandered out of the kitchen, dropping her sketchbook onto the settee as she headed for the front door. It was half past eight as promised. Yatt was laden down, with a large opaque plastic box under one arm, and both a satchel and a laptop carrier slung over his shoulders.

"Good Morning, Bronte," Yatt boomed, far too enthusiastically for the time of day. "Are you still happy for me to study your spider?"

The same man who had been walking his dog yesterday was strolling down the same part of George Street this morning. He glanced up at the house and smirked at Bronte. Bronte gave a sigh, a tight smile then looked back at Yatt. "People are going to think I'm mad."

"I've never found that to be a disadvantage in life."

Yatt swiftly commandeered the kitchen table, busying himself with setting up his laptop, taking out notepads and pens, then snapping off the lid to the plastic container. Bronte watched in bemusement as she waited for the kettle to boil. George jingled out of the mug tree and leapt onto the kitchen table to investigate. Yatt paused in his organisation to watch the giant arachnid. "Is he often in your mugs?"

"He sleeps in there."

"Spiders don't sleep. Well, they're not even supposed to be able to close their eyes."

"Everything must sleep sometimes, mustn't it?"

"Rest certainly, but not necessarily sleep in the sense that you or I do. Spiders have hours of dormancy. They'll get hidden away somewhere and just sit. This is what your mug is, a safe little cave to rest in."

The kettle clicked off the boil.

"Do you want a cup of tea or anything?"

"Yes, tea, thank you. This is the mug where he rests?" Yatt had already taken the mug off its hook. "Did you put this in here? What is it, wool?"

"George put that there himself. He must have pinched it out of my wool bag."

"Such strange behaviour."

George had moved to the window sill and was tapping on the glass.

"He wants to be let out." Bronte looked from George to Yatt. "You're not going to want him to go wandering off today, are you?"

"Maybe later, but this morning I really want to test his cognitive abilities. Problem solving. Don't worry; I've brought some of the things we feed the tarantulas at the university. And I promise not to release a plague of locusts in your house."

Bronte watched with a touch of distaste as he produced an old ice cream tub that looked to be full of drunken oversized grasshoppers. He took one out and threw it to George who nimbly caught it.

"I'll put this in the fridge. It keeps them dozy."

"They're not going to get out?"

"Hardly ever happens. Only once someone found one crawling in their sandwich..." he broke out into a grin. "You'll never know they were there."

She made the tea, then sat back down on her stool to watch the opening pantomime. In fully documenting the entirety of

George's existence, Yatt was starting off with weights and measures, trying to persuade George to stand in the scales, then to flex each leg in turn for measuring, which was easier said than done. George and Yatt began a cautious little dance around one another, never quite sure what the other was about to do. Neither showed any fear, rather just a relaxed bewilderment.

"You've never seen any aggressive behaviour from him?"

"I wouldn't know what that looked like, but I don't suppose so," Bronte said. "Certainly not towards me. I have seen him go for house spiders. Which is fine with me. I can't stand spiders."

Yatt caught her eye at that comment.

"I do realise George is a spider."

"A very oddly formed one. Technically a tarantula, I think. But there's something of his agility and leg formation that makes me think of a huntsman. I would really love to know where he came from. You do hear of spiders coming through with shipping from South America, what with all the fruit imported. Although most are usually spotted before the consumers get their food home. Still, bananas could be a possibility. When did you buy the suspect bananas?"

"That really hot snap we had a few weeks ago. I got them at the shop up on the high street. It's funny, we were having a fly infestation here at the time, then they all seemed to disappear. I had hundreds stuck on this fly paper hanging off the ceiling, then it seemed to be picked clean."

"A readymade larder for the new arrival."

"That wasn't exactly my intention when I put it up." Bronte caught sight of the clock and gulped down the rest of her tea. "I'm going to be late for work; I'll have to head off." She pulled open a kitchen drawer and scrabbling between freezer bags and old tea towels she found a spare set of keys. "If you need to go out."

"Thank you. You're very trusting, Bronte."

"Are you saying I'm a bit dumb?"

"No." He leant back into the chair. "Academics can get a bit insular. We're stuck in our university laboratories and we forget about the real world. I know some of my colleagues the other weekend opened their mouths without thinking. But people aren't worth worrying about."

"I'm not." She said curtly, feeling uncomfortable. "It's fine. I'm fine. Anyway, I've nothing worth stealing."

He lowered his brows. "Are you saying I look like a thief?"

"No, I..."

He started laughing. "Bronte, don't take me seriously."

"I have to go work. If you need to go before I get back, just shove the keys through the letterbox."

"I will probably still be here. Have a good day."

There was rustling in the living room, the sound of books being knocked over as she rushed about. Then she was pulling on her shoes and hurrying out of the front door, her bag hanging open off her arm.

Yatt looked at George. George looked at Yatt.

"Very well, let the games begin. You show me your world."

When Bronte returned home from work, the house was silent. She paused to pick up the post from the doormat, noting that no house keys had been dropped through her letterbox. She loitered in the front entrance, gently pushing the front door to. She almost felt awkward for coming into her own home.

"Hello?"

No answer.

Perhaps he'd gone and just forgotten to post the keys through the letterbox. It was an automatic reaction to simply pocket keys after locking up. She wandered through to the kitchen, where Yatt's laptop was on the table in hibernation mode, along with papers, sticks and other random artefacts. George's mug was empty, but she noted the open kitchen window. George must have gone out. So did that mean Yatt was following him, the two of them making a particularly odd couple roaming the streets of Saltaire? She wasn't even sure where George went when he left the house. Perhaps he just sat in Albert's birch tree and enjoyed the breeze.

Her stomach rumbled and she realised that she needed to eat. Turning the oven on, she got a pan of water on to start boiling, and pulled a frying pan out of the cupboard. She got a bag of minced quorn out of the freezer, then went to another cupboard to look for boxes of chopped tomatoes. When she turned back around George was standing by the kitchen sink.

"Oh, you're back."

George stared morosely back at her.

"Well, I'd better shut the kitchen window." Yatt, wherever he was, wasn't going to be following George that precisely. She walked past George, not particularly distressed by such close quarters with a spider, and shut the kitchen window. She went right around the kitchen table and back to the hob top. She quickly chopped an onion and got it into the frying pan with some oil.

"Good Afternoon!"

Bronte jumped as she was cutting open the bag of quorn.

Yatt had appeared in the now-open back door. He looked eager and full of fresh air, with a large cardboard box tucked under one arm. "George has been showing me the sights of Saltaire. We've had a busy afternoon."

"Oh. Does he go far?"

"A few streets in either direction." He looked to the cardboard box under his arm. "I just need to put this in my car."

And with that he was gone again. George wandered across to the corner of the kitchen where Bronte had various glass jars and jugs filled with different dried pastas. He peered in at a jar, either curious by the curling frozen forms, or catching sight of his own washed out reflection.

Bronte poured the chopped tomatoes over the mince in the frying pan. The water was starting to bubble so she took the lid off the pan. She looked to the jars for spaghetti but saw that the usual jar was empty. She got a fresh pack out of the cupboard then went to the draining board where she had left the scissors.

Cutting open the packet, she pulled out a handful of spaghetti, going back to the hob top to put it into the water. She returned to the packet as George was creeping up to it. Bronte pulled out a single stick of spaghetti and held it up. "Pasta. Where would we be without it?"

She pointed the stick at George, who stepped forward and bit the end. Bronte laughed. "I don't think you're going to find that very tasty." When she went to pull it away she found the spider had latched on to it, and had a surprisingly determined grip. "Okay, you can have that one," she laughed, letting go and watching George swirl it around like an oversized wand.

Without consciously knowing why, she looked back to the living room doorway. Yatt had returned at some point and was leaning in the doorway, watching her and George with a gentle smile on his face. She suddenly felt self conscious and turned back to the sink to pick up the packet of spaghetti. She hovered for a moment or two, not really sure what to do or say next. The weight of observation now hung on every movement. She left George randomly waving the pasta, and put the spaghetti away in a jug.

"I think he may be Italian. He seems very keen on spaghetti."

"Perhaps. My money's on South America."

She went over to the oven to stir the tomatoes and mince together. She suddenly felt that she needed to fill the silence. "I'm always so hungry when I get back from work; it's the first thing I have to do when I get into the house." She looked back at Yatt, a thought suddenly occurring to her. "Oh, I mean, I always make too much when I cook; you're welcome to stay..."

"No," he shook his head. "I want to go back to Leeds. But thank you. I have taken some venom from George and I want to start testing it as soon as possible."

"Venom?"

"All spiders have venom. They have to be able to paralyse their prey."

What with having believed George was imaginary, she hadn't really considered the actual facts. Her mind hadn't acknowledged that he might be capable of acts beyond scaring her with the very fact he was a spider. That George could actually be dangerous, well, it didn't seem credible whilst he was perched by the sink waving a piece of spaghetti in the air.

"Is he dangerous?"

"Of course. If you're a mouse or a bird or an insect. I was most worried about his uriticating bristles, but George doesn't seem to have this ability. I spent some time this morning trying to get him to do it, but his hairs aren't like other tarantulas. I suppose in them being longer and denser, sacrifices have been made."

Bronte just stared at Yatt. "I don't know what you're talking about."

"Tarantulas from South America have these bristles in their abdomen that they can flick out at you, like darts, if they feel threatened. They can cause irritations and problems, especially if you get them in your eyes. Tarantulas from other places; Asia, Africa, Australia, can't do this. But then their venom is stronger."

"So you don't think he's South American?"

"I'm not sure. But the biggest tarantulas come from South America. I'm not sure if he's just a severely mutated tarantula species, or a species that we've never seen before. It still happens even today that new species are discovered."

"He's not going to bite me?"

"I wouldn't have thought so, not unless you provoke him. And you've been living with him for so long now without trouble."

"But he's venomous."

"No healthy person has died from a tarantula bite. It might make you a bit sick, maybe just a rash, or maybe headaches, nausea... There's a tarantula bite from Africa that causes hallucinations. But I want to get the venom sample in the lab. See what we've got."

"Okay." Bronte slowly stirred the contents of the frying pan. She was a little surprised that this wasn't freaking her out more. Living with a creature that could make her ill from a bite. It was the reality of many subconscious fears of the archnophobe. "So will you be coming back to see George?"

He paused a moment, watching her, before choosing to answer. "Yes, I do want to come back. I have a faculty meeting tomorrow morning, so perhaps tomorrow afternoon. Are you working tomorrow?"

"Yes, same hours."

"I'll maybe come at six. I really want to talk to you, about the behaviours you've seen. You've been living with George; you'll know him better than anyone." Yatt finally left his position in the doorway and went to the kitchen table to start packing up. "I'm leaving that tub of crickets in your fridge."

"Oh, you really don't need to."

"If he starts getting hungry or wanting to go out, you can feed him those." He put the laptop away in a bag. "I think it's best that you don't let him out of the house anymore."

Bronte looked mortified. "I shouldn't have let him out? Look, it's not like he's my pet, he just turned up here."

"I know. I'm not accusing you of anything. But we don't know how toxic he is. I doubt he would kill an adult, but what about a child or a cat? If that happened, can you imagine the uproar? And what would happen to you? I don't want you to suffer any repercussions."

"I suppose."

"I've followed him around the locality, seen his haunts and I have also found his larder. You know spiders store their food for later. I've actually emptied it; that was what was in the box. I don't know how happy he will be if he goes out and finds someone has made away with all his treasures."

"I guess."

"I'm going back to Leeds now. Thank you for your hospitality. And I will see you around six tomorrow if that is acceptable?"

"Yes, of course."

"Your keys," he added, putting them on the kitchen table. "Have a pleasant evening."

Bronte walked him out, shut the front door then returned to the kitchen, feeling rather subdued. She looked at George, who let go of the pasta. It hit her that this was only going to be temporary. When Yatt had collected all his notes, he'd be gone. She was beginning to realise that George wouldn't be staying.

Last night's dinner didn't look quite so exciting the following lunchtime, cold and slopped into a reused plastic container from a Chinese takeaway. It made a change from sandwiches, and Bronte was ravenous, wolfing her food down as if she hadn't eaten for a week.

It was quarter past two and she was on a very late lunch. Everyone had seemed to take a longer lunch than usual today. The delays had pushed back the queue of hungry booksellers until it was past the point when Bronte ought to have been returning from her own lunch break and yet she was still to eat.

She had gone out of the mill to sit on a bench in the nearby park and take some fresh air. The bench with the view straight on to the weir had been free when she'd wandered across the bridge, so she'd hurried over to claim her place. Not that she was appreciating the view, for keeping her loose hair out of her dinner whilst trying to get the food into her mouth as quickly as possible was all she could concentrate on.

"Bronte! Mind if I join you?" Eileen appeared with a leftover sandwich from the lunch run at work in her hands. One of the pros of working in a cafe was the free food. "How's it going?"

"I'm starved. I was meant to be on lunch ages ago. How are you?" she managed to get out before putting the last of her vegetarian spaghetti bolognaise in her mouth.

"All right. Nothing too much exciting yet this week. But what about you? Andy said he and Yatt had been over to yours on Sunday."

"Yes, and yesterday he was there with George all day. And supposedly he's back this evening. He wants to know about life with George."

Eileen smiled coyly. "Yes, from what I heard George isn't the only focus of the study."

Bronte looked mortified. "You're not telling me I'm part of the study? He's not writing some paper about mad women who live with spiders."

"Not that I'm aware. Not that I'd really know anything."

"I don't want to become some academic freak show for them all to pick apart. Case study number one." Bronte snapped the lid back onto her empty lunch box and put it into her bag. Both women's' gazes drifted up to the bridge where Paul Warren was sauntering across.

"Afternoon, Paul!" Eileen yelled at him.

Paul broke out into a wide grin, tapped his cap in their direction. Bronte felt herself shrink back into the bench. Please don't come over to talk to us. He left the bridge, jauntily hurrying down the steps, and headed off up along the river away from the weir. She felt her shoulders relax.

Eileen looked mildly put out by the snub, but let it go. "So has he said how long this study is going on for?"

"Who?"

Eileen laughed. "How many men have you got coming over to study George?"

"Oh, yes, sorry," she shook her head. "I don't know. But I don't suppose it'll be that much longer." Bronte shuffled in her seat, not sure if she dared to voice her concerns. "The thing is, he said I shouldn't let George out."

"You let George out?"

"I'm not his keeper."

"But he's a bloody tropical beast."

Bronte felt she was missing the point. "I think he's going to want to take George away."

"And?"

"Well, I..."

"Come one, you don't want George living there forever. I know it's a novelty, but he's a big ugly-arse spider. And you're supposed to be terrified of spiders."

"I don't get other spiders in the house now."

"Bronte, you don't want to end up like one of those mad cat women. But worse. Bronte the mad spider woman."

Bronte held her hands together and looked out at the weir. She felt unsettled but she couldn't put her worry into words. Only that she feared she was going to lose something soon.

"Look, they've got loads of bugs and shit in tanks at the uni. It'll be the best place for him."

"Of course, he hasn't said anything yet."

"Yet," Eileen emphasised. "Seriously, if Yatt hasn't brought it up by the end of the week, I'd start pestering him about it."

Even if she was sure she wanted to give George away, Bronte doubted Yatt was the kind of person who could be pestered into doing anything he didn't want to. Bronte was at home and was staring in the mirror over the mantelpiece whilst brushing her hair. It had been loose all day and had inevitably become tangled. She stared into her reflected eyes and tried to work out what she wanted, but she just looked confused whilst her stomach rumbled. She stopped mid brush and looked at her hair brush in confusion. What was she doing? She never brushed her hair when she got back from work.

When she went into the kitchen, George went straight for the kitchen window and started tapping to be let out.

"No, you're not supposed to go out anymore."

George turned around to see if she was in the room. Big blue eyes asking to be let out.

Bronte looked in the fridge for the crickets Yatt had left. She held the tub in her hand, grimaced at the look of them, and put it back in the fridge. She really didn't think she was up to handling those things.

She went back into the living room and put the CD player on. "Come on, George, if we're not allowed out, let's have the party in here." She found a rock CD and flicked through so the *Ace of Spades* started playing. George scurried across the floor like a giant dismembered hand and scrambled up onto the CD player. He stood and started to thump his abdomen to the beat of the music as the vibrations went up his legs.

Bronte felt her stomach rumble and went into the kitchen to make some food but no sooner had she reached the table then George was back at the window tapping to be let out. She felt like a traitor, and fled to the living room. They'd just have to both listen to rock music and starve.

At half six the doorbell rang. Yatt was waiting on the doorstep in full gleeful volume, carrying a beat up satchel and a plastic bag full of boxes.

"He's not finished all those crickets you left, you know," Bronte said, letting him into the house.

"This isn't for him," Yatt rattled the bag. "This is takeaway. To say thank you for letting me into your home. You eat Chinese, don't you?"

"Oh thank Christ," she burst out, feeling her stomach sing in joy. "I can't go in the kitchen. He keeps wanting to be let out."

"Just give him one of the crickets. I thought you said you had some left."

Bronte grimaced. "I don't want to touch them."

"You're squeamish about bugs?" Yatt laughed. "And this is your housemate?" He looked around the room and caught sight of George pulsating on top of the music speaker. "What the hell is he doing?"

"I thought you knew. I guess he's dancing."

Yatt walked right up to George and peered into the creature's big eyes as if an explanation would given forthwith. "You could call it dancing," he said, not sounding convinced. "He must like the sound pulses. With all those hairs, he must be hypersensitive."

"He seems to prefer something with a good bass line."

Yatt looked back at her and grinned widely. "He has a good choice in music. I'm going to have to film this but I don't have my camera with me today. Will it be okay if I come back tomorrow?"

That's my day off, Bronte thought. "Sure," she said.

"All right, let's get this show on the road." He clapped his hands together. "Let's venture in the kitchen and if he comes begging I'll feed him some crickets."

"Right."

Bronte headed straight into the kitchen, but Yatt hung back. The moment she stepped through the doorway, George leapt off the speaker and fled across the living room floor after her. It was the strangest co-existence he had ever seen. Entering the kitchen, he saw George tapping at the back window, whilst Bronte was determinedly trying to ignore him, sorting out plates and cutlery. Yatt took the cricket tub out of the fridge and threw George a couple of treats.

"What do you want to drink?"

"What have you got?"

"Water, tea, milk..." Bronte crouched down to rifle through a bottom cupboard.

"Is that your wine cellar down there?"

"I'm not a big wine drinker, sorry."

"Neither am I. I'm a Viking you know, we just drink schnapps and vodka and go a bit mad."

Bronte paused and looked up at him. He didn't look as though he needed intoxicating spirits to 'go a bit mad'. "Okay..." she said. Her hand fixed around the neck of a bottle and she pulled it out. "This is a bit heavy for the middle of the week, but I have whiskey."

He looked impressed with this suggestion. "You didn't strike me as a whiskey drinker."

"A very occasional glass." She stood up, looking at the label. She'd not even opened this bottle yet. "It was a present from my brother. He's not really got a talent for presents so we get all kinds of odd things for Christmas."

"I think I'd be very happy with whiskey for my Christmas presents."

Bronte bit her lip and wondered who did buy presents for Yatt. He was without context but he had to have people. For all she knew he could be married with a troop of screaming little mad things back in Leeds, all with red hair and loud voices. She looked back at the bottle. It was Tallisker, which was a distillery on the Isle of Skye. Branwell had given this to her the Christmas just gone. He must have already been scouting out this new job even then.

She took a jug of water with her as she didn't want to wake up with a bad head on her day off. Back in the living room she tried to bring some order to the sketchpads and books on the coffee table, but gave up and dropped them onto the floor for the time being. Plates and glasses were put out, and the food dispensed. Bronte soon retreated to one of the two shabby two-seater settees in the living room, the scent of food torturing her stomach. She couldn't be polite and wait, just had to fill her plate and start. It was bliss to finally eat, to curl up into the sofa and not be on her feet any more.

"You know there's a payback for this food, don't you?"

"Sure, whatever," Bronte muttered, grabbing a couple more prawn crackers. "It's been such a long day and my legs are wrecking. As long as I get to eat, whatever. You want to talk about George."

"I do want to know about George," he started carefully. "I suppose everything you've seen. I think you've been living in a rather unique situation."

"Tell me about it." She took a couple more forkfuls of food before accepting she'd have to slow down and converse. "Where do you want me to start?"

"Do you mind if I record this on my phone?"

"What is this like a police interview?"

"Nothing incriminating. I just can't eat and take notes."

"I guess," she eyed his phone suspiciously, casually thrown out into the middle of the table. Still, it wasn't like she had any secrets or anything of great interest to divulge.

"When did you first notice George was in the house?"

"The first time I saw George?" She leant back into the settee. "Oh, that was back when no one believed me. I saw his legs coming out from behind this painting and I just freaked. I ran to get Albert, and when he took the painting down there was nothing there."

"Why did Albert need to come here?"

"He usually comes over and takes care of the spiders for me. It's just that they're not usually that big." She paused as the sound of clinking ceramics came from the kitchen. George had just gone to bed. "I'm scared of spiders."

"This is the really curious thing about your situation. How are you managing to live like this? Or do you think George has cured you of your fear?"

"No. It still makes my flesh crawl when I see him running about. That eight-legged movement, it's not natural..."

Yatt burst out laughing. "It's very natural. George probably wonders how we cope on just two legs."

"It still makes my flesh crawl. When you came over the other day, when you thought me and Andy were making it up, you let George touch your arm." She shuddered at the memory. "I couldn't do that."

"You've not had George sitting on your shoulder?"

"You must be joking."

"He's been sat on my arm. He's not aggressive, very relaxed."

Bronte felt sick. "You mean all eight legs?"

Yatt shrugged. "Yes, of course. He's just a spider. A very big one, but just a spider. I don't understand why people have this fear."

Bronte mopped up the last of her sauce with rice and pushed it onto her fork. "I couldn't do it," she muttered, putting the food into her mouth.

"So, despite your fear, you are happy to live with George. You've not tried to kill him, and you don't shut the window when he goes out."

"Well, yes, I suppose. I don't know why. I did almost kill him. It was the second time I saw him, he was on the kitchen table and I just freaked. I had the frying pan and I was going to whack him."

"So what stopped you? Did he jump and scare you?"

"No, he looked at me. He must have had his eyes closed, because it was all just brown. And then..." she shrugged. "You've seen his eyes; he does look a bit pathetic. I just couldn't do it."

Yatt shook his head to himself. "That was Andy's theory. All the hair and the big eyes. He's a bit cute."

"I wouldn't call George cute; he's still got quite an ugly creepy face when you look at him."

"Hey!" Yatt looked offended.

"Hey?"

"Have you not really looked at a spider's face? The mandibles, the teeth, the eyes. It's an amazing piece of natural design. They are these highly talented hunters..."

"I've not made spiders my life."

"There is a beauty to them. You just have to look. I think you've seen it. Yesterday George took me on a tour of your house..." His eyes widened, darkening pools. "I was not snooping, please don't worry."

"It's fine, I trust you." She leant forward, picking up the whiskey bottle and snapping it open. "Do you want a drop?"

"I won't say no."

"You'll have to serve yourself; I can't reach your glass."

"I can manage that, thank you." He took the bottle from her. "But what I was trying to say, was that I couldn't help but see your drawings. These black and white paintings of George. They're quite charming. There's real affection for George in there. And you seem quite relaxed to be living in a house with George."

"It's like you said, he's not aggressive."

"No. It's interesting, people have these preconceived ideas, and... oh, this is very good." He stopped as he tasted the smoky whiskey. "I wouldn't say whiskey is usually my first choice, but this is nice."

"It's from Skye, where my brother's moving for the new job. I suspect this has been on his radar for longer than we realised."

"You'll have to go and visit him and get some more."

"I suppose I will." Bronte finished her glass, the wee dram, and sank back into the cushions, feeling the fiery, peaty alcohol burn through her veins. She hadn't really considered it before, but a trip to Scotland wouldn't be such a bad idea. She'd heard Skye was supposed to be a beautiful place. Yatt was talking again, she snapped out of her day dreams.

"... when I was out in the town following him, he was in someone's front garden. An old woman was passing me and she thought he was a flock of sparrows."

"Sorry?" Bronte laughed, thinking she must have misheard. "How could anyone think George is a sparrow? He's far too big."

"He was in the dirt kicking up a lot of dust. You've seen little birds when they do this? They get their arses right down into the dirt to take a bath."

"Yes of course." Bronte took the bottle and refilled her glass. "Wait, you mean George was taking a dust bath?"

"He's a very hairy spider. He's got some little mites on him. I think they are an irritation."

Bronte held her glass on her lap and gazed over at her mantelpiece. So was that where all of her dust had gone? George had been trying to rid himself of mites all over her dusty shelves. "Do I need to get some flea powder?"

"I'll bring something over tomorrow. I want to get in the lab first thing and check the tests on the venom. I'll come back over maybe mid morning. You'll be at work by then I think."

She shook her head. "No, it's a day off tomorrow."

"I can leave it a day if it will disturb you."

"No, it's fine," she waved his concerns off with the half-melted movement of the slightly tipsy. She took another drink. "Don't want to leave the itchy spider waiting. Especially if he's not allowed out now. So when you were following him, what were you after? Testing his navigation skills, seeing how far he could go?"

"Partly that. But I wanted to make sure I knew everywhere he had been. Just to make sure there's no permanent damage."

Bronte was thinking. The comment about damage passed her by. She looked up at Yatt, who appeared to be very comfortable in her other settee. "Did you go to the park?"

"The park?"

"Over the river. Down the hill and over the river. That way." She swept her arm out in the general direction.

"No, we didn't cross any water. Why?"

"We did go to the park once."

"He followed you?"

"Hitched a ride in my bag, really. I sat in the park and did some drawings. George had a bit of a run around, then we came home."

Yatt started laughing. "You took a spider to the park?"

"Sure, why not?" She smiled.

"This has been the strangest week I've had in a long time. Okay, we have to go to the park tomorrow."

"I'll drink to that."

The evening continued through a drunken warm fug, talking about spiders, about the things that George had done and odd behaviours that made Bronte wonder. George remained in his tea mug. The sunlight turned yellow, lowering and slanting through the sky and the front window. The lighting level lowered. Bronte started to feel sleepy, gradually slipping closer into the curves of the sofa as if she might never get back out.

Yatt pulled himself out of the soft, warn settee before he got too comfortable and fell asleep. He was just at a pleasant level of inebriation, not so that he would appear drunk, but rather relaxed, talkative. He picked up his phone, turned off the recording function and checked the time. "I'm not going to be able to drive back to Leeds tonight."

"Oh," Bronte raised her eyebrows.

"Wee bit too much of the good stuff," he said, making a poor imitation of a Scotsman.

"Right." She shuffled in the sofa as if trying to wake up. She thought of upstairs. There was the spare room. There was a spare bed. Really she barely knew the man and he did look a bit crazy, but that was only his outer appearance, and she felt that she could implicitly trust him. She'd managed with George; a wild-eyed Icelander ought to be no problem. "You could..."

"When is the last train to Leeds?" he asked at the same time.

"Oh." She stopped in the offer. Maybe he'd get the wrong idea if she said he could stay over, and then he'd feel embarrassed and have to politely turn her down. Not that she had intended to suggest anything other than the spare room. "Twenty to eleven. What's the time now?"

"Almost half ten." He answered, standing up to his full height and putting his phone in his back pocket. The upward stretch was a reminder of his height, suddenly looming over her and casting a long shadow across the room. "I'll get the train back; I'll pick up my car tomorrow. I'm keen to get in the lab first thing. I'll come back mid morning, if that's okay with you."

"Of course." Bronte suddenly felt awkwardly sober. "The train's just a couple of minutes from here."

"Yes, George took me on quite a tour; I've got enough time to catch the train." He smiled across at her. "Thank you for the hospitality, Bronte."

"It's nothing."

"I'll see you tomorrow."

She loitered at the door and watched him stride down the street in the dusk, and around the corner out of sight. With a sigh, she shut and locked the door. She went into the kitchen and drank a pint of water, a habit after any alcohol that she'd stuck to religiously since a particularly bad drinking night in her university days that had taken days to get over. Turning off the lights, she wandered upstairs. She avoided her line of sight in the mirror when she brushed her teeth, then walked across the landing in the dark to her bedroom. Flicking on the bedside lamp, she took off her clothes, dropping them onto the floor, then pulled on her pyjama trousers and a vest top and hopped into bed. It was warm, so she kicked the duvet down, lay on her back and turned out the light. Closed her eyes and expected to go to sleep. Her brain was whirring, and the sleepy whiskey had reversed its effects now. She was restless, laying on one side then the other, thumping pillows and kicking at the duvet. It was past midnight by the time she managed to drift off to sleep.

"Things cannot continue as they are."

Bronte raised her eyebrows and felt her body shrink back into itself. This was the opening to an uncomfortable conversation. It was the standard line to kick-start the break up chat, but given that they weren't in a relationship, she didn't know what was coming. Or rather she did, but she didn't want to talk about it.

Having walked through the park, crashing through flower beds and carefully planned shrubberies to keep track of George, Yatt had returned to the bench where Bronte was idly sketching. He seemed satisfied that he knew what the spider was doing, and had an easy confidence that they'd be able to collect the arachnid when it was time to leave. Now he leant back into the bench, laying an arm along the back rest in a proprietal fashion. He let the statement settle between them, knowing with increasing certainty that the longer Bronte didn't react, the more she knew what he was talking about. This was a conversation he hadn't been looking forward to, and the more time he spent in her house, the worse he felt about it.

Bronte eventually looked up and begrudgingly met his stare. "I don't know what you're talking about."

"You do. George can't be left running around free any more. I did mention this to you before."

"George just happened to pick my house to live in. It's not like he's my pet or anything. I'm not responsible for him."

"I don't think that statement would stand up in court."

"I can't put him in a cage."

"It would have to be a terrarium; like a giant fish tank. A cage would be no good. He'd probably get out between the bars."

"Whatever. I can't lock him up. He's all over the place; always running about. He's not some pet to sit on a rock in a tank and look pretty... not that he's pretty anyway. He's a wild animal."

Yatt wobbled his head, looking to disagree with that notion. "If we were living in Brazil now, I would agree with you. George is a wild creature. But this is Great Britain, and here he is an invasive species. He's doing all kinds of damage to the natural eco system."

Bronte looked away from him and gazed down the main path. There were shrubs and trees planted up on each side, and she soon spotted George motionless under an overhanging leaf of a large hosta. Close by in the middle of the footpath a couple of old women were stood gossiping. "I'm not putting him in a tank."

"That's fine; I will. We have a really good one at the university, recently emptied."

"So you and your students can dissect him?"

"No one's going to dissect him. I aim for him to live a long life. It will be a good comparison. We have an African tarantula that lives in the department. She's called Doris."

"And she's in a tank."

"Most of the time, but we do let her out in the lab for the students to see."

Bronte's grip tightened around the top of her sketchpad, feeling the coiled wire binding press into the palm of her hand. It hadn't been a life ambition to live with spiders; in fact she'd always dreamed of a spider-free home. But now that George was living in the mug tree, it was as though he'd always been there. The house would be silent without that gentle tinkling as he climbed in and out of his ceramic bed. It would just be Bronte, alone in the kitchen with all her silly drawings.

Yatt took his arm off the back of the bench and took a piece of folder paper out of his jacket pocket. Unfolding the paper, he leaned forward to push himself into her periphery view. "You're not letting George out of the house, so he won't know that I've emptied his larder. Do you want to know what I found in there?"

Bronte pursed her lips together.

"Five chaffinches, three field mice, one shrew, one house sparrow, one greenfinch, one little bird I've been informed is a goldfinch, and a greater spotted woodpecker."

Her eyes widened at the final item on the list. "A woodpecker?"

"The local wildlife doesn't know George is a danger. How do you think bird populations will cope in the long run? And when he's eaten his way through that, what will he go for next?"

"I guess."

"I'll come over tomorrow with a little tank, get him over to the university. You can't live like this indefinitely. With a giant spider running amok in your house, begging to be let out every time you go into the kitchen."

Bronte didn't have anything to say. She gazed wistfully up the path to where George was crouched in readiness. Something in the opposite flower bed had caught the attention of his big blue eyes. All of sudden he streaked out from his cover, a brown flash nipping across the footpath, unashamedly between the old women's legs, and into the undergrowth at the other side.

The old women shrieked in unison. "Jesus, Mary, Joseph," one of them burst out. "Mabel, did you see the size of that squirrel?"

She broke out into a smile tinged with sadness, and looked back at Yatt. "Okay. Tomorrow." She dropped her bag onto the ground, gaping open, and stood up. "George?" she shouted as if calling a dog to heel. "Time to go."

George knew that something was afoot. The atmosphere had changed; something sparked in the air. The tone of sounds had shifted. He did not understand that he was going to be forcibly evicted the next day, in fact the signals George was picking up on suggested something quite different. He stood on the speaker and wavered slightly to the music. The vibrations from this track didn't do all that much, barely making the hairs on his legs quiver. Normally he would have wandered off to do a quick patrol of the property in case any tasty morsels had strolled in. But this evening he was unsettled, and like a safety blanket, the stereo speaker felt like a secure place to loiter. So he stood, his sombre blue eyes looking out into the room. If he had been able to cry, if his brain had contained a complex emotional response and if he had known what would happen tomorrow afternoon, he would have shed a few tears.

Yatt and Bronte had returned to their respective settees in the living room and were working through the second half of the whiskey bottle. Yatt seemed to be resistant to actually going home, and Bronte really didn't want him to leave. If she could have stopped time, just kept this evening on repeat forever, she would have been quite content.

And so they slouched back in cushions, and drank and chattered. Spiders were a starting point, as many a great conversation could state, but the themes soon drifted into more autobiographical subjects. Bronte was surprised to learn that there was more beneath the loner wild-man of Siberia look than she might have first presumed. Yatt was one of those well-travelled, well-read people who had really gotten out into the world and lived. Like her brother, he would have an autobiography worth writing when he was old. From his home town in northern Iceland, he'd headed to Copenhagen for his first degree before then moving to Brazil for further academic study. He'd lived there for well over six years, getting his doctorate under his belt, as well as a three year marriage that had ended gradually for her as the novelty of a Viking husband had paled against the attentions of local men, and suddenly for him who had just assumed marriage meant constant loyalty. Those were his naively youthful days, when he was beardless and innocent looking. He admitted the long trips into the jungle looking for spiders on his own probably hadn't helped matters. But it was never pleasant to learn it was over, returning home to find your wife and a stranger at the peak of an acrobatic routine that ought to have been dangerous given how much sweat they were producing. The marriage was over, the divorce was quick and Yatt fled back to the northlands to live in a remote cabin in Iceland, writing his book on the spiders of South America. He let the beard grow and cultivated a wild look whilst perfecting the art of self sufficiency. Having convinced himself the human race was a bunch of bastards, he then heard of a teaching post at Leeds in the UK and thought perhaps it was time to try living on a different island.

It was quite a story. Granted he was older than her, forty to her thirty one. It was only natural he would have done more in life but Bronte thought over what she'd acomplished in her first thirty odd years of life. Her life story was going to be a much shorter book. Probably not on the best seller lists. She picked up her glass and took a reasonable sip of whiskey. She looked over at Yatt, who was watching George, and as she felt the alcohol burn a warming path down her throat. Something in her centre seemed to melt and fall out.

"Did you not miss them?"

Yatt looked at her and raised his eyebrows questioningly.

"The spiders? I don't suppose you have any in Iceland."

"Of course we do. There are spiders wherever you are. But on Iceland they're not very big. You have a lot more variety here in the UK."

"Still, it can't be that exciting compared to some of the places you've been." She looked over at the stereo where George seemed to be staring back at her in a rather affronted manner. It was a point well made.

Yatt smiled thoughtfully to himself. "I'm quite happy with the discoveries I've made here."

Bronte picked up the whiskey bottle to refill her glass, but discovered it was now empty. "All gone," she sighed. She pulled herself up from the sofa, her movements slow and languid. Her mind felt muddled.

"I'm sorry we've drunk all your whiskey," Yatt said, not sounding all that sorry.

"No matter." Bronte stood in the room gripping the bottle by the neck as if she were about to make a speech. "It's meant to be drunk, not just looked at."

A silence of waiting settled in the room.

Yatt was the first to break it. "I should head off. I'll get the train back and sort my car out tomorrow. Are you working tomorrow?"

"Yes, but I don't start till eleven. It's probably best if you take George whilst I'm out. I don't think I want to be there." She wandered into the kitchen. "You'll have to take his mug. I don't want it anymore." Flicking on the light, she caught sight of the clock. "It's ten to twelve."

"Shit, I hadn't realised it was so late. When is the last train?"

"About an hour ago."

"Oh, I..."

"It's fine," she said, wandering back into the living room, warmed by alcohol. "You can stay in the spare room."

"I feel I've imposed on your hospitality..."

"You haven't."

George dropped down from the stereo and with a scuttling of many feet across the carpet, ran for the kitchen. There was the gentle tinkling of porcelain as he climbed into his favourite mug.

"Come on," Bronte said. "Let's head upstairs."

Despite the late night and the alcohol, Bronte was awake at her usual time in the early morning. She couldn't sleep, and had pulled herself out of bed and headed in the direction of the kitchen with the intention of getting tea ready. She got as far as the kitchen doorway, and leaning against the doorframe gazed at the gentle morning light coming through the window and was lost to her thoughts.

Last night had been strange. It had taken her a long time to drift off. She'd probably only had a couple of hours sleep, so it was a godsend she'd remembered to drink a pint of water or she wouldn't be functioning at all today.

After George had made a dash for the kitchen, she and Yatt had headed upstairs. There had been a politely awkward moment on the landing, then they had retreated to their respective rooms. Bronte had changed into her pyjama trousers and vest top, and flopped into her bed. Her chest had felt pent up, begging for a release. She had stared at the ceiling, her arms and hair splayed out across the mattress. Tomorrow it would all end. No more George. No more Yatt. Just silence and Bronte. Still pent up. Solitary. This really hadn't worked out how she wanted but she hadn't felt capable of putting what was racing through her system into appropriate words. It was an old fear of being laughed at. Don't put yourself out there, and then you'll never run that risk.

She had felt her eyes well up with tears. She had wiped at her eyes with the back of her hand, then twisted in bed to look at the wall. This was the joining wall that met with the spare bedroom. Knowing the layout of her furniture, she had been conscious of the fact that her bed was pressed up against the wall, just as the spare single bed, where Yatt now lay, was touching the other side. Bronte had pressed her hand flat against the wall and closed her eyes. He wouldn't know.

She picked up a paintbrush from the edge of the kitchen worktop and twisted her loose hair up off her neck. Tendrils escaped and dropped down against her back. Bronte folded her arms, let a sigh out and watched the flickering light move as the breeze moved through the birch foliage outside.

The quiet was pounding. It made her want to shout out everything that was running through her mind. Her very veins pulsed. On the outside she looked like a languid, barely moving mill pond. Lost in idle thoughts. Solitary.

Something brushed against her bare shoulder, stopping at the strap of her top. Bronte didn't outwardly react, for a moment wondering if she had imagined the sensation. The air had changed. It had electrified. She could feel the temperature rising from a heat source just behind her. Her chest felt ready to burst. Desire was immobilising her legs to the point she wasn't sure if she would be able to move. The fingertip was still resting against her skin. Poised. Then with the eloquence of a piano chord being played, three more fingers tapped down against her shoulder.

Please keep our breathing under control, she begged her lungs. Pushing against the doorframe for momentum, she turned around a full hundred and eighty degrees. The hand fell away from her skin, and in turning around on the spot, she almost knocked her forehead against Yatt's chin for he was standing so close. The air between them was compacted. She just wanted to push her way through the final distance and merge. Neither of them had yet to speak. Bronte looked up and met his eye.

The doorbell rang.

The was a moment, a merest fraction of a second, then Yatt balled up a fist and knocked against the wall before pulling away. Bronte opened her mouth as if to protest, her face distraught. He was picking up his jacket from the back of the settee and walking for the door. Bronte followed him, wanting to grab handfuls of his shirt and drag him back into the moment she had been prepared to submerge herself in. The door was opening and Yatt was walking out of her home.

Bronte hurried after him but something held her on the threshold. Her mind started to race in time with the rest of the world. Albert, waiting on the doorstep, looked mildly bemused and curious about the large red-haired bearded man he had seen before, now leaving Bronte's home at this time in the morning.

Albert held up a couple of envelopes as Bronte watched over his shoulder. Yatt strode a short distance down the footpath and got into his car.

"These were delivered to my house," Albert said. "I was meaning to bring them round yesterday evening and forgot."

So you decided to bring my post in the wee small hours of the morning? Bronte thought. She could have throttled Albert as the sound of a car engine, Yatt's car engine, started and joined the chorus of bird song. Over the other side of the road she saw Paul Warren jauntily striding up the road. From another one night stand. He winked at her.

"Thought you might want them."

"Right, thank you," Bronte said distractedly, taking the letters off him.

"Did I...?"

Yatt was driving away. Around the corner and gone.

There was a thud on the front window. Both Bronte and Albert peered around to see George stretched out as far as his legs would go across the glass, his mouth seemingly pressed up as if to make faces at passers by.

"What's up with him?"

"I have to get ready for work," Bronte declared, even though it was a late start this morning and she didn't need to be there until eleven.

Shutting the door on Albert, she stood in the front entrance, listening to him mutter and shuffle off back down her garden path. She stared down at her post, feeling as though she wanted to gasp or sob, but instead simply stuck in numbed horror. He had walked away. She would go to work. He would come to the house, take George, and that would be that. No more visits from Yatt. She was going to implode.

The doorbell rang again. Bronte glared at the door. Had Albert remembered a fucking parcel he'd taken for her a few days ago and thought she might be in desperate need of first thing in the morning before most normal people even thought about getting out of bed? Another pointless interruption when those damned letters could have waited or just been shoved through the letterbox.

She wrenched open the front door, needing a release and ready to give her retired neighbour an ear bashing of nothing but hysterics.

There was no Albert. Yatt stood on the doorstep, looking slightly embarrassed. He put his hands up as if to say these things can't be helped. "I don't do things like that."

What was 'that' supposed to refer to? He didn't like to seduce women from whom he was trying to take mutated giant tarantulas? Bronte felt her heart break, the impact pressing out at her ribcage. She didn't know whether to cry, drop to the floor or hit him. Instead she merely stared, meeting his gaze.

"No," he told her, catching a look of uncertainty. Taking her by the shoulders, he backed her into the house, stepping inside and shutting the door behind him. "I don't know why I just walked out."

Bronte looked from one hand on her shoulder to the other then back to his face. There wasn't anything to say. He moved his hands to cup her face and kissed her hard on her mouth. The first moan escaped her mouth, in relief at the release, and her hands went to his shoulders and neck, pulling him down into her. They staggered awkwardly for a moment before sinking down onto the bottom of the staircase. The edge of a step was uncomfortably pressing into the small of her back, the carpeting against rubbing her skin as her vest top was wrenched off, but she was too focused in getting his shirt off him. He begrudgingly took his hands off her just long enough to slip through the sleeves before he was back on her flesh. Her entire body was pulsating, desperately screaming for him to come into her.

George strolled back into the kitchen, relieved that the electric atmosphere had broken. And in his simplistic spider-way of thinking, assumed that would be the end of that.

But that was not quite the end of that. In truth it was only the beginning of the rest of time.

Five months later and George was perfectly settled in his new environment. It had taken quite a time of breaking in. The security of familiar territory beyond the rim of his sleeping mug had changed beyond all recognition. Worse was how his freedom to roam had diminished. He now lived in a particularly warm environment, where the temperature and humidity could never be faulted. There were rocks and pieces of wood to clamber over, great glossy leaves to sit beneath, and naturally the cool smooth confines of the mug, now resting in a spread of sand. Food virtually strolled straight into his mouth in this world and he wanted for nothing. Nothing apart from a range to explore, for this new world was restricted by transparent walls, so that he could seemingly climb up the air and reach the dark sky above.

Outside of his warm home there was an odd world, self contained with no access to the wilderness. Far across the way, he learned with time, there was another transparent container where a much smaller creature like himself lived. A blind creature from all he could see, for there were no visible eyes.

Quite regularly he was lifted out of his home, often by the wild creature with so much red hair, or by others, and allowed to run around the larger environment. There were other such creatures watching, some shrieking and scuttling away from him. Such great lolloping things, as if he was a danger. Many an occasion there was just him and the red haired one in the room, and they would sit at a table and the man would throw George crickets and other treats to eat.

For several months he did not see the long haired woman he had lived with, to the point he wondered if she had died, and then almost forgot about her. She who had called him George, for in this new place they used a different sound.

One day he had been out in front of a woman with pink pigtails and a selection of gawky youths, who all gasped as he moved his eyes across their array of faces. He was fed, allowed to run about and hop from desk to desk for a little time before being shepherded back into his tank. He was just about to settle down for a rest when he heard his old name being uttered. The name she had used. He crawled up to the wall and stared out.

"You should have come earlier."

"I just didn't know how I'd feel about it, seeing him boxed up," Bronte said. "And he's over here?" She walked up to the long tank and bent forward to look in. George stood tentatively on a sawn log, staring back up at her. Quite healthy and well fed, she assumed, for a spider. She was still fearful of the comparatively tiny creatures that had repopulated her house, and the sight of a giant spider ought to send her screaming, but she couldn't help but smile when she met George's eyes. "It was bloody weird those first few weeks after you'd taken him."

"I know, your house almost looked sane," Yatt laughed. "But we've had other things to distract ourselves."

Bronte smiled coyly. "Indeed." In truth she had wanted to come and check up on George a long time before now, but she hadn't been ready to come to the university with Yatt. There was a period of near disbelief, and thinking that if she went out into the real world with Yatt, somehow it would all blow away into the fantasy it felt like. But Yatt didn't disappear, and just as she got used to the fact that George no longer lived in her home, it felt as though Yatt always had.

She stretched back up, and looked along the length of the tank. It wasn't the same as being a free creature, but it was as good as he could get, not being a native species. Bronte ran a hand along the length of the tank lid, then tapped a sticker with a name on it. "Was this the previous resident?" She twisted to look back at Yatt, who was beginning to look sheepish. "Georgina?"

"That's the thing I never found the right way to tell you," he started.

"What have you done?"

"Nothing. You were so attached to your spider, and so convinced about certain facts, I didn't want to break the picture whilst you were living together."

"So you're calling him Georgina now?"

"It's not a he."

"George is a she?" she said, her tone almost suggesting it was impossible. Truly? All that time it had been the two girls living together. "I had no idea."

"Spiders aren't easy to sex if you don't know them."

"I just assumed because he... I mean she, was so big and hairy..."

"Ah, well," Yatt nodded sagely. "Appearances can be deceiving."